Passed Through the Window

On My Way to Life...

By D Rae

PublishAmerica
Baltimore

© 2004 by D Rae.
All rights reserved. No part of this book may be reproduced, stored in a retrieval system or transmitted in any form or by any means without the prior written permission of the publishers, except by a reviewer who may quote brief passages in a review to be printed in a newspaper, magazine or journal.

First printing

This is a story based on fact as well as fiction. Any resemblance to any other character, place or thing, as well as any resemblance to an actual person, living or dead, is purely coincidental and was unintended by the author.

ISBN: 1-4137-5055-9
PUBLISHED BY PUBLISHAMERICA, LLLP
www.publishamerica.com
Baltimore

Printed in the United States of America

Acknowledgments:

There can be a time in our lives when we either back away from diversity or go forward with the strength to challenge it head-on. Thanks to my family, I am able to tell this story of my life on the farm—the good times as well as the challenging. Without their support I would feel most uncomfortable writing the detailed facts that are the backbone of this novel.

I remember many good friends who were unable to cope with the pressure they suffered at the hands of their lending institutions during those difficult farming years. I also remember many friends and family members who have succumbed to the terrible disease of Alzheimer's; two dear cousins as well. It is difficult to watch good minds deteriorate to what appears to be a vegetative state.

Especially, thank you to a good friend for helping me recognize there was a story for me to tell, also that I had the ability to tell it.

Introduction

Life growing up on a family farm, silently preserved in the memories of an elderly mother, is the basis for this novel. Even though physically strong, her slowly deteriorating mental condition mandated the change to nursing home care throughout her remaining time on earth. Her family had been trapped with the difficult decision of keeping their loved one with them in their home or taking her to a facility better suited for her constant, crucial care. Even though she realized these young people who had been caring for her were very important in her life, she hadn't the capacity to communicate her thoughts to them. By gazing through the only window in her room, this beloved mother recalled the happy days of youth on her family farm, only to be shadowed with sorrow and depression. Not until she passed on to eternity did she once again find the happiness she knew as a child.

The difficulty of watching this once bright, alert mind slowly fade into a childlike, helpless being became more difficult for them each ensuing day. Trying to understand this terrible disease, trying to reason its attachment to some individuals yet not others became a constant stress-trigger for her family. Questions without answers were constantly in the thoughts of her children: Why had their mother been chosen to suffer with this horrible ailment, and why did two of her cousins succumb to the same disease? Is this a coincidence? I think that's very unlikely. Is it hereditary? If so, what would cause it to surface in this generation only? Has our water or soil been intoxicated with harmful chemicals to the detriment of our immune systems? Could it be the caustic chemicals that were first made available to farmers during this era, so new that their use wasn't always applied with caution?

Since land has transferred from small family farms to large corporate farming during the past two decades, has it made the use of pesticides and herbicides indispensable? Even university mentors have been fast to recommend larger farming units with less soil preparation and more chemical use. It remains to be seen if this direction will ultimately be the best choice. Will there be a day when our soil becomes sour and barren, when chemicals must once again be replaced with labor? When that happens, will irrepressible illnesses become less prevalent?

Do we know if Alzheimer's patients are capable of inner feelings and detailed recollections even though unable to communicate them? We don't, but recent studies show this to be a possibility. There are some who believe, as I do, that "inner feelings" are the language of the soul, however readers of this novel are left to their own elucidation.

A Daughter's Lament

We drove our conservative gray van into the parking area reserved for "visitors." Once there, we were immediately greeted by an employee who was out enjoying a walk in the warm afternoon sun. Before we had a chance to park in one of the marked areas, she politely directed us over to the adjacent lot which was the "residents only" parking area. Since that entrance remains open during daylight hours, we were allowed to drive right on through the massive, black iron gate. As if to further point us in the direction we were to follow, rows of stately pine trees cast their shadows from one side of the concrete drive to the other. A groundskeeper off to the right of the path was busy trimming spent yellow blossoms from the shrubs that had just finished their spring showing. He looked up as we approached, stopped his work long enough to smile, then motioned us on up the pathway toward a large three-story building. More beautiful evergreens lined this path as well, not as tall as the previous ones but still showing the same majestic stature. We slowly approached the building. As we passed from behind each ensuing tree, the large building became closer and closer.

Even driving as slowly as we could, we found ourselves all too soon in the area marked "unloading zone for residents." It seemed so final. The dark red brick walls of the large building made a picture-perfect backdrop for two large stone pots overflowing with buttercup yellow flowers. The three of us walked toward the building, trying to keep our thoughts condensed to the building and the flowers—anything except why we were there.

As we walked forward on through the large wooden doors, we were greeted by the home administrator. After a minute or two of small talk about our trip and, of course, the weather (a typical conversation for this Midwestern area of the country), she escorted us a short distance down the hall until we came to the room that was readied for Mother to begin her new life. It was obvious how apprehensive she was. She did not want to leave our home where she had been living for the past few years any more than we wanted her to leave. But, after several family discussions, it seemed to be the only way for her to receive the care she desperately needed at this point in her life. Their medical supervision will be so much more help than we are capable of providing even though we have tried so very hard. I know she is fully aware of this even in her failing state, but it was hard for everyone— hard for her and hard for us.

We went into her room for the first time. A perky young high school girl dressed in the typical red and white uniform brought in a food tray. "Are you hungry after your long trip? I have some snacks and lemonade for you" she said to Mother as she smiled her big welcoming smile. Mom nibbled on a cracker a little bit and sipped part of her cold lemonade, but most everything stayed on the tray to be picked up later by her new young friend. The three of us visited there in this unfamiliar room for another hour trying to avoid anything negative in our conversation, trying to avoid the words that none of us wanted to say. This was her new home; this would be her home during her remaining years. Our idle chit-chat was more about the room, the decorations, the walls, the drapes—"nice drapes," the bed, "is it comfortable? what pretty linen, what a nice view out the window," obviously trying to keep comments positive during the time we spent with her before saying "Goodbye" and it was time for us to leave. I'm sure she is aware of the situation even though unable to express her thoughts with words. She is trying so hard to hide the tears swelling within her eyes as we said our goodbyes. As the door closed behind us, we could see her forced but comforting smile. It is so typical—she is being left in this strange place, yet she is still trying to comfort us. Even though I am confident it is the best thing to do, leaving her was the most difficult moment I have ever experienced.

We slowly walked back down the hallway, back through the large wooden doors, and back down the long, winding path. The perfectly placed shadows were now a blur across the pathway without identifiable form. I thought to myself, *That's how today has been— a blur, without appearance or form.*

From the time we got to our car and all during the drive home, there was minimal conversation. Again, only comments regarding the room, the view out the window, the bedding and how friendly the sweet young girl was trying to be, but neither of us mentioned the inevitable comments about Mother's remaining days there in that room she will now call home.

When we arrived back from what seemed to be an exceptionally long trip home, it was time to prepare the evening meal. I don't remember what I prepared; it didn't matter. "It's time to eat," I told my husband as I placed the food on the table. When we sat down for our meal, my eyes couldn't help but focus on the one empty space. I couldn't help but wonder what Mother was doing back in her new surroundings. What was she thinking? Was she adjusting to her room? Was she eating her evening meal? Or, was she just picking at it as she did her refreshments?

Love Makes the World Go 'Round

Dear ones, please, shed not a tear for me. Even through the haze of my own tears, I could sense their sadness as they walked out the door. They have been so good to me and I love them dearly. I will try hard to make my days here optimistic—anything to keep these wonderful people from further worry. I only wish I could remember more about them. I wish I could talk to them and tell them what I feel in my heart; what I do know and what I do remember—what I would like to say, but just can't communicate. I hope they understand.

In this small room I am now to call my home, the surroundings will soon become familiar. One-room surroundings should not take long. There is a bed, dresser, closet and small bathroom—that's all.

As I sat down on my bed, hoping to relax after an emotionally weary day, my eyes soon focused on the one small window. It is the only area of my new room that doesn't confine me. As I gaze through this only opening to the world around me, I see cornfields in the distance. That familiar sight helps comfort my immediate feeling of fear and loneliness as I allow my thoughts to race back to my childhood where cornfields were always visible throughout our farming community. Straight rows of corn set apart the best farmer in the area. Many nights my family would drive up and down the dusty country roads to note which farmer had the straightest rows of corn.

Of course, my dad always thought he did, and he pretty much was right. I'm sure planting with horses helped since it took horses longer to get out of line than it did the powerful tractors that were to be the way of the future. I sat there on the bed for several minutes just looking out my window and thinking about corn planting; how I loved sitting on my dad's lap as he maneuvered the corn planter through the fields. I'm not sure if I was in his way, but I loved it and he didn't seem to complain about it either.

Horse-drawn corn planter

There was a tranquil quiet when riding on the planter with only the sound of the *click, click, click* of the seed corn dropping down through the planter chamber and into the ground. The smell of sweaty horses in the hot sun was a constant reminder of just how hard they were working. Once in a great while my dad would shout at one of the horses, reminding them to hold up their share of the teamwork. "Gee" or "Haw" (left or right) he occasionally called out to the team as he gently tugged the long leather straps he held in his callused, suntanned hands. If he got really upset with one of them he would call out his (or her) name in a loud, chastising voice. Team horses always had short names like "Babe" or "Jake" that were easily heard and recognized. As if in response, they would occasionally whinny back to us.

When my dad got tired or really bored he would sing. Of course, with me being his only audience, and not an especially astute critic, he could sing as loud as he wanted and as off-key as he was capable of doing. His favorite songs were hymns since that was mostly what he knew—the very favorite that I loved to hear him sing, was "That Old Time Religion." If I got tired or bored during the long day of planting, he would let me lay down at the edge of the field so I could take a short nap before returning to the planter. The sun-warmed soil provided a cozy bed for me.

Very few planes flew overhead, and no cars—or at least very seldom would we see a car on the road. If we did, we always knew it was one of the neighbors. Once in a while, if we happened to be at the end of the fence row and our next door neighbor just happened to also be at the end of his fence row, we stopped for a short visit. Those brief visits were always about the progress of planting, the ground condition and, of course, the weather. The three of us would look over to the western sky making our prediction for that night—rain or no rain? Were we going to have a good season? Were we going to have a dry year? A wet year? The crop year was never expected to be just right when you lived on a farm. There usually was mention of the family and how they are doing—the wife, the kids. After a short visit, my dad and I would get back on the planter to continue planting the long, straight rows of corn.

In the fall when corn was picked by hand the horses, as well as their owners, put in a long day of work. Our team pulled the large wagons back and forth between the corn rows while a "husker" (that's what we called him) walked alongside, snapping the yellow ears away from the mother corn stalks, then tossing them high over the wagon side and into the box. Breaking the ear from the stalk was a trick in itself since it required a quick, twisting motion of the wrist. A good husker could actually husk one hundred bushels in a big, full day. We had a husker come up from Missouri one year who was a one hundred-bushel-a-day husker. He was the only person I had ever watched move through the corn rows that fast. By the time he unloaded the wagons to ready them for the next day he had put in one long, tiring day. Metal rims edging the large wooden wheels made narrow tracks in the dirt as the wagon was pulled forward between the rows. Large back boards were attached on each side of the wagon so the ears of corn would hit them first before bouncing on down into the wagon base.

Our horses were brushed, fed, watered and put in the barn for a well-deserved night of rest. It was fun to brush the large, beautiful white horses even though I found them intimidating when they shifted their large bodies back and forth letting me know just how anxious they were to bed down for the night. Since workhorses eventually needed to be replaced, some of the mares were allowed to have babies during the early part of the year. By the time fieldwork was in full action, the foals were old enough to follow by their mother's side as she worked the fields. When the foals became hungry, lunchtime required a short rest period before resuming work.

Since we fed out most of our corn, my dad or my uncle would take the train into Chicago to buy young feeder calves, then have them shipped back by train. Thousands of calves quickly went through the auction ring in a day's time, so the speed of the auctioneer could make any slip in bidding cost the purchaser several hundred dollars. Bidding became an art, an art both my dad and my uncle had artfully mastered and enjoyed even though it could be stressful at the time. The young calves were shipped in boxcars back to the nearest town with available holding pens. Once calves were watered, fed and rested, they were trucked out to our farm. The same system took place when the fattened cattle reached a desired weight, only in reverse order—shipped back to Chicago for sale. Before trucks were available, cattle had to be driven to the nearest rail station by men on horseback. That was before my time, but I'm sorry I missed it— know it would have been great fun.

Cattle penned in Chicago Stock Yards

Ears of corn were kept either on the ground or in wooden cribs. Corncribs were made up of four-inch boards placed in a slanted position with two-inch spaces and, like the barns, painted red. The spaced boards allowed for air circulation, keeping corn dry during the wet winter months that followed. Any corn left after our livestock was sold was shelled off of the cobs and ground up fine for feeding chickens. The bare cobs then were good for bedding or heat, especially since they had a high percentage of the husks still attached. Some families even made jelly out of the corncobs, but we never did. It actually was quite good, tasting much like apple jelly. We had enough apple trees to pretty much keep us in jelly without that additional work.

We also had grapes and apricots and pears and cherries and peaches and rhubarb and strawberries and raspberries and sometimes gooseberries when we went to the timber to pick them, so we didn't have a shortage of fruit to make jams and jellies. While we were on our mushroom hunting trips to the timber we noted where the gooseberry patches were located so we could go back later for picking.

Searching out those special mushrooms hidden in the underbrush was a spring excursion—some years successful and some years not so good. The hunt was worth every effort when we found enough for at least two or three meals. Mushrooms had to be rinsed several times because dirt and ants could hide under their rough texture. Once they were clean, we patted them with lots of flour and fried them in lots of butter with extra salt and pepper—we had ourselves a mushroom feast. They were a delicacy we had at least once each spring unless dry, cool weather conditions prevented them from growing. The mushroom hiding place was kept a secret as if it were a new gold mine recently discovered by prospectors. Any other food was shared with neighbors when we had more than we needed for canning, but not the mushrooms.

Listen to Your Elders

After emigrating from Germany, my great granddad was the first member of our family to settle in Madison County. My granddad was born one year later in 1852. When he was thirty-one years old, he married my grandmother. They, too, raised their family on this farm, continuing to help Great Granddad farm the land. Then my dad, along with my uncle, stayed and farmed the same land to help out my granddad. It was a family tradition.

Mom's parents

Dad's parents

My grandmother on Mom's side of the family was born in Germany in 1855 and came with her parents to Iowa when she was four years old. Like many families, they settled in Clayton County, Iowa, but when land values skyrocketed after the Civil War they found less expensive land in Madison County.

My other grandmother's family, after coming from Germany, settled in the northern part of Iowa as well. One of Grandma's young brothers died during the long boat trip crossing the Atlantic Ocean. This strong German settlement remains in Jefferson Township where many family members still farm the land.

Our mother told us on several pertinent occasions how Granddad was strict with her and her siblings. She said that when they were children, meals were for eating only. Granddad allowed no arguments, fighting, or even giggling. If they did, they were asked to leave the table without eating. I always kept that in mind—I didn't want any rules like that coming back to haunt me! Her subtle reminders were enough.

Actually, we behaved most of the time during dinner anyway.

One of the few rules we were required to follow was to be quiet when the news came on. When Dad turned up the radio volume we knew it was time to "shush."

My older sister cut notches in the oilcloth table cover, each notch matching the size she summed up for each one of us. Of course, my notch was very small all the way up to Dad's, which was quite large. I, on the other hand, only wrote the names of everyone on the tablecloth so we each knew where we were supposed to sit. I got very annoyed when people didn't sit where they were supposed to. My first (and last) cutting experience was whacking up the monopoly game because my sisters wouldn't let me play.

The only grandparent (my mother's mother) I knew lived until 1953. The other three had passed away before I was born. I felt bad about it because I would like to have known them—from what I heard they were pretty interesting. The grandma I did know was such a petite person with snow-white hair pulled back behind her head in a tiny, neat bun. On her 80th birthday she showed us how she could bend over and place the palms of her hands flat on the floor in front of her. That was something the rest of the family, even though younger, could not do. She obviously was the ancestor who passed her flexibility on to me since I could do it easily.

Christmas day at Grandma's house was a grand event our entire family looked forward to since it gave us a chance to see all of our relatives. Grandma gave presents to everyone—her children, their husbands and children, the grandchildren's spouses and children, and even their families. The normal count was about ninety of us, each receiving one of her loving gifts. We usually found a pair of socks or mittens in our package—nothing expensive. Since she didn't live far away, my mom would help her with the purchases, then they would individually wrap each gift. That was a chore for both, but Grandma loved doing it, and there was no convincing her otherwise.

After dinners at her house everyone played games—usually the older kids would play card games of some type. Our younger group especially liked to get out her stereoptic viewer. She also had several kaleidoscopes to keep us fascinated during the afternoon. Not having enough chairs for everyone to sit at the table to eat, we kids used it as our excuse to sit on the stairs away from the adults. Our system was simple—plate on one step and our feet on the lower one. It worked out great for us although I'm sure we made a mess for Grandma. She didn't care she just loved having us there.

Thanksgiving dinners were the same, although not quite as many family members attended. Grandma always cooked the large turkey in her old wood-burning stove. Water for dinner was pumped through the small cistern pump that sat on the wet-sink counter. Everyone brought food to go along with the turkey so there was never any shortage of delicious food. We just expected that there would be snow on the ground by Thanksgiving and there usually was, and if not before, it would arrive that day. It was a rule. We kids could go outside to play after dinner if the weather permitted, if not, we just played inside. The adults were much happier when we could play outside.

There were only a few in our age group as most of our cousins were older. There were usually only six of us, so we had to stick together. We would entertain ourselves in a variety of ways, but one of our favorites was by simply placing a blanket over a card table. It was our own little tent where we felt privacy and safety away from the older kids.

I have many of my grandmother's traits. In addition to her limberness, I also have her features and hair composition. Like Grandma's, my hair has always been light and fine. When I was very young, I was called a "towhead" but I never knew what that meant, or if it was a good thing or a bad thing. I guessed good, because the sunshine made my hair glisten with an almost snow-white appearance. Grandma's hair was white, too, long and straight to her waist. After she washed it, she combed it over her right shoulder, wrapped it around her left hand, twisted it into a bun with her right hand and held it in place with an elegant hairpin. I always watched with awe at the speed she could do it. My hair was just as straight, but not as long. It either hung straight down or was braided into pig tails.

Seldom was it curled. I did have it curled professionally when I was eight years old, though.

Our small town nearby had a beauty shop, and since my mother didn't like my hair hanging straight in my eyes, she convinced me to go have "the perm." What an experience! When I walked into the room, the first thing I saw was a huge, intimidating machine with at least fifty wires attached. The wires hung down using some kind of mechanism that could adjust their length necessary to reach my head. The beautician meticulously separated my hair into as many little sections as she could, wound each little section up on a tiny little metal roller, then attached each little roller to one of those hanging electrical wires. After my entire head had wires attached all over, the heat was turned on and left for what was probably thirty minutes (seemed like hours for me to sit still that long), then the wires were removed. When the metal curlers were also taken out, I could finally see what was accomplished during all of this time I had wasted. I was horrified, only I didn't let it show. My hair looked like I had stuck my finger up into one of those electrical units. I had curls, and I mean *curls*, all over my head. They weren't just curls; I had one big, frizzy head. That was the last time I ever succumbed to a perm, especially in a professional setting. I have since had a few home perms where I could keep more control over my fate, but not many. Like Grandma's, my hair was so fine I always ended up with frizzy curls. Well, I went home from my harrowing experience at the beauty shop and I brushed and brushed and I brushed some more when my mother wasn't looking, trying to get my hair back straight again. Mother wasn't exactly happy with me when she found out I had used the scissors to cut away some of my unwanted curls. "It cost money," she let me know in her outburst, but what was I to do? The money was already spent; I couldn't do anything about that and, I still had the frizzle job—minus what I had trimmed off.

Thankfully, home perms became pretty popular after that time. I helped give them to my mother and sisters at least once a year when we were all at home. We had our own little smelly beauty shop right there in our kitchen. Since Mother couldn't raise her right arm up to care for her own hair, I helped her with washing and curling each week. Washing hair wasn't a daily cleaning routine, but a weekly routine on Saturday mornings. During the winter when we had fresh snow, we would gather buckets of snow to melt on the stove, then wash our hair in the nice, soft snow water. Actually, baths weren't a daily routine either before we had the automatic running water, especially hot water. The term "Saturday Night Bath" wasn't far off. When it was hot during the summer months we would bring a (clean) stock tank in from the barn, fill it with water, and play in it during the day. The water was solar heated, but since that was an uncommon term, we said simply that the sun warmed it. That made up for our bath, only on a daily basis.

After playing all week, barefoot and in play clothes, Sundays were a different story. Dress attire was required to go to church and Sunday school. That was okay since each spring we each got a new Easter outfit, from the undergarments to the dress (and, yes, it was a dress). The only strings attached to the new wardrobe were that we had darned well better be ready when Dad yelled at us, "Are you ready for church?" He wasn't overly strict, but we learned to recognize the stern look and the commanding tone in his voice when something was really important like going to church on Sunday. With a family of all females he couldn't very well let us "dawdle" around. My dressing habits were formed during those nice summer days when I could time my dressing down to the minute so I didn't miss much outdoor play, yet could still be ready when he called.

Many Hands Make Light Work

My dad, his brothers and their sister always referred to my granddad as "The Boss," never "Dad" so we of course never heard him say "Father." This always amazed me since I'm sure it would be a cold day in heck (we weren't allowed to say hell) before I could get by calling my dad "The Boss." I often wondered where that came from because my granddad wasn't a large, intimidating man at all. In fact, Grandma was the larger of the two. Dad said she could eat like ten threshers at dinner, and that she started the sweet corn season by eating only eight ears the first day, then working her way up from there. They called her "Ma" which I thought pretty brave, but back then I guess it wasn't that unusual. Even after my grandparents died, they were referred to as "Ma" and "The Boss." Everyone in Dad's family had nicknames, so I'm not sure I ever did know their real names.

A large family of boys provided my grandparents with a heavy-duty work force along with some heavy-duty mischief. My Aunt Bea, the only girl in the family, took a lot of abuse from her brothers. One time during the cold winter months, my aunt's devoted brothers "suggested" she stick her tongue on the cold pump handle which, of course, she did. Yes, her wet tongue did stick, permanently, until a very disgusted mother poured water on the pump handle to release an extremely sore tongue.

Keeping the boys busy was no doubt necessary for the safety and sanity of everyone else in the family. What a scene it must have been when they were all young and overly active. The big, typical square farmhouse provided a racetrack for them to run from room to room, round and round throughout the entire house. It's amazing the house survived.

Actually, the first house didn't survive—it burned to the ground. It was rebuilt however, on the same sight on the hillside next to one of the many famous covered bridges in our county. This same bridge, McBride Bridge, was set on fire by an arsonist in the 1990s. The many people who had connections to the popular relic felt it a real tragedy and historical loss. In earlier times, most area families referred to this bridge as the Burger Bridge since there were so many of the Burger family farming land adjacent to the bridge. When a small post office named McBride was constructed in that area, the McBride name was attached to the bridge to remain throughout history.

A few years after rebuilding the farmhouse, my grandparents decided to move to a more level piece of land they owned. Up until that time, they always wanted to keep the level ground for farming with the buildings constructed on less valuable, hilly land. After years of doing chores on the slopes, this new level area became more inviting. The new sight was two miles from where their new house now stood, so it was a major undertaking to move it to its new location. The boys in the family jacked up the house, framed it well to steady it, and moved it up to the new area with horses. That was done during the winter months while the ground was frozen. Since the new sight was bare, the boys dug up large trees with balls of frozen ground still attached to the root system, then hauled them up to the new yard for planting. By digging a large hole in the frozen ground for placement of the new transplants, then watering them well, the transplants were a success.

House ready to move

With that big, healthy start, all of the trees survived and grew well. The elm trees had to be taken down when the Dutch Elm disease hit them in the 1960s, but all of the maple and pine trees continued to grow.

A new barn and other farm buildings needed to be constructed at the new sight just as soon as time permitted. Since Uncle Joe had been out in the western part of the United States constructing barns during the time he wasn't driving the huge steam engine tractors in the wheat fields, he knew exactly what to do when it came to building barns. After sawing all of the wood to length during the winter months and stacking it close to its future building sight, they were able to construct the large hip-roof barn in the early spring.

Building the barn

Dad's oldest brother was the only one of the family to go through college. After graduation from Iowa State College he became the first county agent (as they were called then) in the state. He was involved in the first vaccination practices for livestock as well as several other new experimental techniques for helping the farmers become more productive. Even though not in college, all of the brothers had college course study books and manuals that they referenced—mostly regarding farm animals and crops.

Another brother was also in the war along with Dad. Because of his flat feet, the Army wouldn't let Dad serve in heavy fighting, so he had to serve his time as a cook. The other brothers stayed home to help with the farm work.

Uncle Joe was the one boy in the family who enjoyed traveling throughout the rest of the country. In addition to living out West, he was planning a trip to Alaska during the Gold Rush but something happened to keep him home instead. He did, however, go to Mexico during the Revolution. It was pretty scary to hear him tell about it. He always told us that one of his cousins was married to the leader, Pancho Villa. I never did know if he was telling the truth or just seeing how much he could make up that we would still believe. This lady's picture was printed in the news later, so maybe he did tell the truth. Of course, even the Western part of the United States hadn't been settled long in those years, so it was still pretty wild.

Bullet holes during the Revolution

Uncle Joe didn't marry until he was in his later years, so up until that time he lived in a small house in the back part of our yard, but he ate most of his meals with us. That made him a constant part of our family, but even so, he never talked much about himself. As a self-taught carpenter, he spent a great deal of time building and repairing things around our farm. His shop was full of interesting things, especially to a bright-eyed young tagalong tomboy. I watched him enough to know how to use most of the tools. The electrical stuff was off limits to me, but when he was gone or busy I could use the handsaws and hammers as long as I put them away and kept them clean. I couldn't use any good lumber, but scraps were fair game; that, and wooden crates our summer canning fruit came in. Canning the fruit was just a necessary, boring chore to get to the good stuff—the lumber. You would think my constant tagging along would get on his nerves, but he really never told me to get lost. His only reprimand when I was doing something I shouldn't was, "You dassn't do that" and I no longer did. No way would I, or any one who knew him, alienate this great supplier of candy. He had lemon drops or pink mint candy with him at all times or, if not in his pockets, available in his car. Those were his favorites.

Uncle Joe had a regulation Army Jeep, too. What fun! When our other vehicles couldn't make it through the deep snow, we would get to drive the Jeep. His Jeep didn't have any top though so it wasn't exactly a winter vehicle, but when we wanted to go to town we ignored such minor inconveniences. An endless supply of candy, plus riding in an open top Jeep—we couldn't ask for more than that.

Uncle Joe was always buying something whether he needed it or not. He had boxes of socks, shirts and handkerchiefs that he never did use. Since he kept all of the machinery and buildings in repair as well as building new wagons and other farm necessities, he had a good excuse to supply his workshop with new saws, hammers, or anything else he thought was badly needed. I loved to watch him work with the tools, and once in a great while I would get to help, or at least I thought I was helping. He kept everything on the farm freshly painted to preserve the wood and, since he seemed to have a passion for what we all called tobacco brown paint, everything he painted was brown.

His first project for our yard was building birdhouses—wren houses to be exact, since a family of wrens was visiting our yard looking for a nesting place. They picked the right yard to call home with Joe around. Of course, the wren houses were built to exact dimensions with the entrance the exact size of a quarter, and, of course, painted the famous tobacco brown color. The wrens had homes all over our yard as well as the entire neighborhood.

One spring my mother purchased a climbing rose bush that needed something for support. As usual, she called on Uncle Joe to build her something. He designed and built a tall and extremely sturdy trellis, anchored it to a fence post and, what else, painted it tobacco brown. Even though she had one climbing rose, she ended up with several of these trellises. It became a challenge for her to find something to grow on each of them. Nobody complained; we were always happy to have his help, even though it was a family joke.

Being a bachelor, Uncle Joe didn't have a lot of expenses and he was able to save more money than most farmers. He was always willing to share what he had and was always good to support every cause, especially the local church.

We considered our indoor bathroom heaven on earth when we were fortunate to have one installed. Until then, we had the normal outdoor facility, or the "outhouse," at the end of our yard. Again, Uncle Joe built us a very special facility (as facilities go) that wasn't even painted brown, but gray. Since I was small, he constructed a "three-holer" with my tiny seat being in the middle between two larger seats. It was complete with a stack of old papers and catalogues that we could use for tissue paper. At least it wasn't corncobs; we could be thankful for that. Since it was eighty feet from our house, it seemed like a long trip during the winter when the sky was dark. Going out there was one of the last things we had to do before going to bed. Being so scared of the owls in the trees, I would run as fast as I could back to the house. The hoot owls made a haunting, scary "hoot" but the screech owls made a terrible screechy noise that made my spine shiver. I know they intentionally waited until I came out the door so they could scare the daylights out of me in that pitch black darkness. In the cold winter months the owl noises weren't so prevalent, but by then it was so cold that I still ran. There was never any loafing on the way back from the outside toilet no matter what time of year it was.

Beauty Is In the Eye of the Beholder

My dad called Uncle Joe "Bagley" (one of those nicknames again), but his real name was Leroy. Anyway, Joe/Bagley/Leroy came home from a trip to pick up supplies one day and told us about buying Christmas presents for some young children. He had seen three little boys looking in the store window drooling over a toy truck. Of course, he stopped to ask them what they were looking at. When they told him about the toy truck he said, "Let's go inside and see if we can't buy it"—which he did. I'm not sure who was more excited– the boys or my uncle. He didn't know them, and they never did know who he was, but that wasn't important. It had made him feel so good. He was still chuckling about their excitement when he got home.

Another day he came into our house wearing a big smile and said in his slow, country slang, "I bought me a birthday present today. You better come out to the car and see what I got." Well, aside from the fact that it was the first we were aware it was his birthday, and I wasn't real excited about seeing *his* present, to humor him I, along with my sisters, went out to his car. There it was. A brand-new shiny bicycle. "WOW!" That was a red-letter day for us since we were sure it wasn't for him. It was our very first bicycle. It was *his* birthday, so he bought *us* the bike—a really nice bike, too. It had a basket on the front, and a seat on the back fender so a guest could ride along. That guest usually was me since I was the youngest and not big enough to ride by myself at that point. I only hoped that whoever was the captain of the ship knew what they were doing and not going so fast that we would wreck. It didn't take my sisters long to learn how to ride, but I must have scratched my knees and stubbed my toes a jillion times before I mastered the art.

I was allowed to kick off my shoes and go barefoot during the summer, so it was inevitable that riding a bike was going to be hard on my feet. If cloth shoes had been available maybe wearing shoes wouldn't have been such a drag—and probably saved me lots of stubbed toes. I was always stubbing them on something, usually on the concrete sidewalk.

There was no such thing as training wheels on bicycles, but even if there had been I wouldn't have used them. I'd sooner suffer the bruises than be anywhere close to being called a sissy. But this was the most beautiful bike I had ever seen; a real bright sky blue color with silver trim in all the right places. Since my legs were still a little too short, when I did try to ride, I had to push the pedals with my toes. Riding a bicycle on gravel was risky anyway since loose gravel could cause nasty falls when the tires spun sideways. Plus, a fall on gravel really hurt. Kids with iodine-covered skinned knees were a common sight. The other major problem with bikes in those days was that clothing could easily get caught in the chain running alongside of the pedals. The kids in the know would either roll up their pant leg or tie them back some way to keep them out of the chain.

After I did get big enough to ride by myself, I had more than a few accidents before I learned to be careful of not only the chain, but also the loose gravel. Bicycles were handy for carrying snacks or water out to the field. Maybe that's the reason he bought us the bike. Anyway, it was for our benefit since at least we didn't have to walk to the fields anymore. Walking was a way of life though, and the three mile hike to school, or walking out to our fields, was customary. During threshing season, before having our bike, we would often ride a horse out to the fields, but other times we just walked.

Since I was such a tomboy, tagging along after my dad was what I did best. It also included going out with the threshing crew when I got the chance. That wasn't very often since it was considered much too dangerous. What a thrill it was though to stand on the top of the big threshing machine as it vibrated violently with each bite of oat bundle it swallowed. The yellow oat chaff would stick to my sweaty, tan body in the hot summer, but I never even complained. I never even complained about the hot metal on the bottom of my bare feet. If I wasn't tough enough to take it, I would have to stay up in the yard. No, not me—that was stuff my sisters could handle.

Sawing lumber for the barn

Oat bundles ready for threshing

My sisters deserved to stay at the house since they teased me every chance they got. As long as I stayed outside I didn't have to worry about them. All wasn't clear outside though either since "Bud" was out there. Bud (his real name was Gerald) loved to tease me just as much as my sisters did—if not more. He was almost a bigger challenge.

Bud and his wife, Ruth, came to our place when I was two years old to help my dad and uncle with the farm work, and they stayed until I was in my teens. They became close family friends as well during that time. A book could be written about Bud and his fine art of "teasery." Since I was so young and eager to learn everything I could, he was obliged to help me out by teasing the daylights out of me.

My tomboy life kept me outside with the men and underfoot all summer long, so some of the teasing may have been to discourage my presence. It didn't—it just made me more intrigued.

It took me a long time to figure out how Bud could pull his thumb off like he did, but once I figured it out everyone from then on saw my thumb come off at least once. And, the amazement of smoke coming out of his mouth in circles? I was awestruck. Since nobody in our family smoked, the smoke itself was different—the rings of smoke were just plain fascinating. Bud thought it was funny to see me try it, only to cough and spit instead. He did let me roll his cigarettes using the quaint little machine he had. The idea was to put a piece of paper in the machine, pour just the right amount of tobacco out of the can (this was the tricky part), moisten the edge of the paper and roll it up into a smooth, neat cigarette. I thought it was fun, plus he got his cigarettes rolled so it was a win-win deal for both of us. Since I spent so much time at their house, I guess he thought I should do something constructive.

One day when I went out to the field where the men were working, Bud called me over and handed me four of the cutest little creatures I had ever seen, then told me that they were baby rabbits. With a sincere look of honesty, he suggested I take them into the house to show my mom. Of course, I did. Pleased with my new pets, I carried those babies right into the house to show my mother, only to have her yell at me to "Get those mice out of the house." Well, I ended up in trouble over it, Bud had a good laugh, and he had fooled me again.

Bud was always there to help with chores. Even with all of the trouble I could find by myself, he usually helped me find more. He loved to squirt me with milk when he was milking—I don't know why—probably just to get me out of his way. He would always try to hit my mouth (and sometimes successfully) with the milk. Hot milk at that point was not at all appetizing, which didn't help my dislike for drinking milk already. The only way my mother could get me to consume the milk she thought I should have was either through gravy (which I loved) or milk in everything from juice to coffee. When it was the coffee trick, it was mostly milk with very little coffee—just enough flavor to fool me.

By the time Bud and Ruth had a baby of their own for me to educate, I was well learned in the fine art of teasing "Bud style." I was relieved to have somebody around that was younger. Their baby boy learned so much from me, which made me oh, so proud. Usually when I taught him something he would repeat it back in baby talk. I thought that was hilarious. One verse he learned was: "I had a little pig, I fed him in a trough, Him got so fat, Him tail pop off." Of course that was his version. What little piano I was good enough to play entertained him as well. "Bill Grogan's Goat" was his favorite song:

> *Bill Grogan's goat was feeling fine, ate three red shirts from off the line. Bill took a stick, gave him a whack and tied him to the railroad track. The whistle blew, the train drew nigh, Bill Grogan's goat was doomed to die. But, he gave three groans of awful pain, coughed up the shirts and flagged the train.*

Then he would just laugh and laugh and want me to play and sing it again.

Bud and Ruth had a niece come visit one summer who I considered to be really cool. Even though she came over to visit with my sisters, who were nearer her age, I tagged along and picked up on all the new, hip ideas I could. I learned from her how unworldly it was to eat toast with hot chocolate for breakfast. Her cool way was to dunk plain bread and butter in the hot chocolate. I must have eaten that for years after she left. Eggs, which I would never have considered eating unless cooked to rock stage, she ate soft and runny to the point where the eggs were all over her plate. They didn't get to stay that way long because of the old bread and butter dunking trick that again came into play. Oh, I thought she was a whole new world that had come to visit, and, if I remember right, she also brought us the mumps. I recovered from the mumps long before I got over that new life she brought to our farm.

For some reason we had a big, old, fat steer that was so tame he would allow Bud to ride on his back. Bud was the only one brave enough to ride, but the old steer didn't seem to mind at all. That's probably where I got the idea to try and ride the baby calves we had, since I hadn't been to a rodeo and, of course, had no TV to view anything like that.

When the baby calves were big enough for me to handle, I would put a halter on them (actually a long rope) and drag them around to break them to lead. Then when they got strong enough to hold me I would try to ride them. They were just small dairy calves with not much meat on them so staying on their narrow, skinny backs was a trick—a lot more difficult than sitting on a big, wide-backed, fat steer. Actually, it was a trick I didn't master well at all.

I wonder if this experience may have helped (or hindered) my 4-H calf showing. I loved the work of caring for my calf, but when it came time for the sale I decided it wasn't going to happen. It did happen, but it wasn't me who led my calf through the sale ring. I wanted to keep him for a pet, so I was nowhere to be found at the time. That was the last year my dad let me have a calf project.

You Can't Spoil a Rotten Egg

I hate to leave this comfort zone I've found through my small window, but I have a few things left to unpack. Most can go in dresser drawers, with the exception of my pretty blue dress that I'll hang in the closet. Just as I finished unpacking my last essentials and neatly placing them on the bathroom vanity, an attendant stopped by to see if I was getting settled. I nodded to her and smiled as if things were fine…

She reminded me, "Dinner will be served in forty-five minutes. Would you like us to take you down to the banquet room or would you prefer to have it brought to your room?" Not that I really wanted food at all, but she can tell I'm content just staying in my room. She went on her way. I'm happy she is gone so I can go back to my view out the window. This small window is soon becoming my friend in an otherwise strange and unfamiliar place I am to call my home, my last home. In a way, I am thankful they brought me here so I won't be a burden to anyone. But already I am wondering what is going on outside of this room—what am I missing? Oh, I see some children riding their bikes past my window; one boy is carrying a basketball in one hand while steering with the other. Now they see me in my window and wave a friendly 'hello'—how nice of them. Since it's late in the afternoon, I assume they are on their way home from a neighborhood basketball game. That group of boys will be ready for a big nourishing meal when they get there.

PASSED THROUGH THE WINDOW ON MY WAY TO LIFE...

Seeing these young energetic boys makes me think of the homemade basketball hoop my dad and uncle had installed for my sisters and me. It was simply a round hoop made of heavy wire and fastened to an electric pole we had in our rock driveway, but it served its purpose and we were happy to have it. Most kids didn't even have that. I'm not at all sure where our basketball came from, but my uncle probably bought it for us so we could shoot baskets.

When I got a little older, but was still in grade school, Uncle Joe built me a playhouse. It wasn't just any playhouse either—it was really a hog shed. Although he built several hog houses for the protection of our pigs, this one was special. He painted the inside as well as the outside, installed electricity and even a floor. I thought it was just about the best playhouse in the world, and for a tomboy that was saying a lot. He even put it in our back yard to make it handy for me. Maybe they were trying to "ladylike" me—I don't know. I added some curtains and then some homemade furniture that I made out of those valuable fruit crates. I loved to build things out of them, and since it was the only wood I was allowed to use, I made the best of it. Once my uncle was okay with me using his tools out in the shed, I could make all kinds of things.

I think he actually got a kick out of my carpentry skills. I made suitcases, desks, chairs; anything I thought I needed. The suitcases were latched with a narrow piece of leather pushed over a nail and painted with some of that leftover tobacco brown paint. I made them for travel, or just in case I felt like running away from home. That actually happened a few times, but since my mother always told me a stranger would pick me up, and would no doubt release me when it got daylight and they saw what they had, I didn't run far. Apparently that discouraged me from actually trying it often. Besides, when I did try, I only got down the road a quarter of a mile before going back home. Mom wasn't worried, in fact, as much trouble as I could cause, she may not have missed me, especially when I couldn't think of anything else to do except start digging a fish pond in our yard. I always wanted a fish pond, but just when it seemed to be getting a nice size, I would get caught—then I'd have to fill all of the dirt back in again.

My other pastime was trying to get up on the clothesline to see if I could walk it like a tight rope. It was much too loose, plus the wire wasn't very wide, but I didn't know at the time that it was supposed to be wide. Apparently I had attended a circus and saw the high wire act. Since it was so far away I didn't notice that they weren't using just a plain clothesline wire. I thought for sure I could do it too if I could just get myself up there to get started. I worked and worked at it but never did get it accomplished. Every time I got myself pulled up, I fell back off.

I had every kind of yard swing one could dream up—I think it was a challenge for Dad to see if he could build one I was afraid of. The typical board seat swing was my first. It hung from a tree branch by putting a rope on each side of the board. This was okay, but pretty boring. I went from that to a single rope that held an old tire. This was more fun since I could twist it up and go dizzy by letting it unwind at a rapid speed. After that was a bag of tightly packed straw. It was also held by one rope and did pretty much the same thing as the tire. The best thing about it was that I could mount it by jumping on the top from a running start. Once I found out how much fun that was I got the stepladder out so I could climb up to the top of the ladder and then jump onto the swinging straw sack. This was the best. To make it even more challenging and dangerous, my uncle welded two large barrels together and cut out holes for steps so I could use it instead of the ladder. I loved that swing—it was the ultimate. I also had just the rope once the bag rotted and broke apart. I tossed the bag away and tied several knots in the rope at different heights so I could grab on anywhere. Amazingly, I never did break any bones, or fall off for that matter. Since the tree limb was thirty feet off the ground, my swings could go much higher than a normal swing.

About the time I was seven years old and had bugged my parents enough, I got to take my first train ride. They took me to the station in our local small town and put me on by myself so I could go visit my cousin. I thought the train would never get there. It made two stops during this ten mile trip, and at each one I asked the conductor if this was where I was to get off. He even brought me a pillow and blanket to use, hoping it would keep me content. After what I thought was the longest ride possible, I arrived and was met by my cousin. We had so much fun that week. I got my first taste of store-bought bread (Colonial) and it was such a hit with me I went home raving about it. It was so much softer and whiter than any I had eaten at home, since all we had was homemade bread.

At the end of the week, my parents came over to get me and had Sunday dinner with my aunt and uncle. I'm not sure why they let me ride the train by myself, but I assume they thought it would be a good experience for me. Plus they were tired of hearing me beg to go see my cousin sometime—one of my very best and most favorite cousins.

One year when I was very small, an airplane landed in our local town. It had two large motors, was noisy inside as well as outside, and resembled the few planes we would see fly over our farm. This one had landed on a grass runway (a hay field) so it could take the local people for rides around the area. Of course, our family had to go check this out since none of us had ever ridden in an airplane. I was only about three years old but thought it was absolutely great. I couldn't get over seeing the tiny houses and trees and people and animals as I looked out the window. I talked about seeing little cars and tiny people for months after. This outwardly cumbersome plane lumbered along so slowly, which was great for viewing out the window. Neither did it fly very high, but high enough to make everything on the ground appear small. It was a new and great experience. In fact, that was the best flying experience of my life. When I was ten, my uncle took me with him to fly over some extensive flooding down in the southern part of the state. I was small enough to ride in the baggage area (sideways) which wasn't good for my stomach. Plus, it had the smell of a new plane, which was an additional problem. By the time we returned to the airport, I was so sick to my stomach. It's a good thing I waited until I got out of his new plane, or the pilot wouldn't have liked me too much.

When I got older, school activities took more time, and I became bored with my playhouse, so it was returned to its original purpose of protecting the pigs. The electricity was removed, but the pigs living in it must have thought they had a pretty special hotel anyway—they just didn't need the electric lights.

You Can Lead a Horse to Water, but You Can't Make Him Drink

I don't suppose I will ever see a horse or a pony out my window. It would be great if I did, but you just don't see ponies anymore unless you are at one of the events such as county or state fairs.

As it happened, the very first neighbor I remember was also my very first friend. Dale lived about a half mile down the road—just the right distance for a day of play. It didn't matter that he was a boy—it was all the better because we liked the same things. Now the big plus was that he did have a horse to ride, and at that time I didn't. It was not just a pony either; he had a full-fledged riding horse.

This horse didn't happen to come equipped with a saddle, which was probably just as well, even though it made our boarding more difficult. The best way we found was to get old (and I'm sure she was) Cricket over by the fence close enough so we could jump on and hope she stood still during the time we were airborne. Actually, the poor horse was probably too old to move that fast.

Threshing time gave us an excellent excuse for horseback riding all day long since we were the "official" water haulers to the men working out in the fields of grain. No other chores were as important or as much fun. Sometimes when he had cousins visit we would get as many as four of us on Cricket, even though the one on the tail end didn't have much traction.

The first riding pony my sisters and I had was a beautiful light brown with a gold mane and tail. We brought him home in our stock truck and unloaded him; all of us more and more anxious to ride our new pony. We couldn't wait. My sisters, of course, took their turns first since they were the oldest. When it was finally my turn, wouldn't you know it, he immediately threw me right off onto the ground. I'm sure that was the last time I trusted him enough to ride since there were no second chances in my book. He bucked me off once—that was it.

Now Silver was whole other story. He was the best pony a person could ever ask for, except for having a mind of his own and pretty much doing what he wanted. But at least he never did buck me off. Even if he had it wouldn't have hurt since he was such a small pony. His very favorite thing to do was stop real sudden so I would go off over his neck, but he always waited for me to get back on. I think it was sort of a game with him however, we understood each other about that. Silver was one of the best bargaining pitches I ever made to my dad. My personal approach for his purchase was followed up with a strongly convincing business letter that worked to perfection.

I wanted Silver so bad that I wrote this business proposition including every reason I could think of to buy him. Neither my letter composition or my spelling was very accomplished at that time, but my ingenuity was pretty good. I had folded the paper up like a letter and on the front written my dad's full given name and address.

> *Dear Pete (this was my dad's nickname):*
> *I like Silver a lot. I will try to get to riding him to school. I think if Evens come up and ride him a lot, I will get used to him. Can we go down and get Valda tonight? Its class time so I'll finish after class. Well class is over and I can*

finish. But Betty is rattlen off and I can't right hardly. Oh dear! Joe put her foot in the mouse trap. And I really jumped. As I was saying, I wonder if Donnie would have to come up. I soppose she would. Three would be to many and both would want to ride, then none of us could ride. I am glad its mudy, because if it was dric they would want to ride the bysickle, and now they couldn't. We ride him up to the school house and back and get him use to it and me used to it. Well its noon and I can't think of any thing so I had better close.
    P.S. GoodBye

    Well, no surprise to anyone, I got Silver. I may have been just a little bit spoiled by my dad since I was the youngest and his only hope for a son. When I was born a girl he was probably disappointed, but I made up for it by being his tomboy. I was born at home in the hottest weather of the summer, and it cost a whole $51.00 for the doctor to come out and deliver me. What a bargain. Well, Silver was just as much fun as I had predicted. I rode him all over the neighborhood. As I had bargained with Dad in my business proposition, "he is really gentle plus I could ride him to school." We did have one big problem with this set up; every morning I would ride him to school, but every afternoon when I expected to ride him home, he had already gone on ahead of me. There just seemed to be no way to keep him at school, no matter what we tried.
    I rode Silver all summer, every chance I could get. I even turned him into a trick pony; I went off over his head (sometimes planned), off the tail, off the sides, under the belly—he took it like a trooper. I never did have a saddle that would fit him so all of my riding was bareback. Silver and I appeared in one parade; after that we participated in one riding competition. We were second in the competition, but of course I (and my dad) always thought we should have been first. The boy who beat me used a saddle.
    My only other opportunity to ride in an actual horse show was

when I was older. One of my friends offered up his horse for me to take into the show arena. Being the vulnerable person that I was, I took him up on the offer. Hadn't I learned anything during those years growing up? Well, that had to be the funniest sight anyone could have imagined. There was no controlling that horse's speed. We passed every other horse in the ring several times before, thankfully, the class ended and we raced out of the gate. He was no Silver, that was for sure.

I hope somebody is taking good care of Silver for me. I wouldn't like for him to go hungry while I'm gone.

My only other great business enterprise was my pet lamb. I always wanted a lamb, but we didn't raise any sheep, so one of our neighbors, knowing my desire, gave me a baby orphaned lamb. I fed that baby lamb with a bottle for several weeks, raised him until he was pretty big, big enough to be ornery and chase me. I then sold the lamb to my dad. Anytime I needed money after that sale, I sold Dad the same lamb again. It was a money making proposition for me, and Dad was having the fun of giving me money and having me ask for it. I must have sold him that lamb a dozen times.

When we had baby pigs at our farm there would be one or maybe two that were smaller than the others. They were called "runts." Since they were too small to fight for food at their regular food station, we would take them into the house and hand feed them with a bottle until they got big enough to eat solid food. They were fun to play with during the time we cared for them and became like pets before we turned them back out with the other pigs. It was the same with baby calves. Once in a great while we would need to take a baby calf into the house to get warm and get some extra nourishment. It was usually when they were born in cold, wet weather. We didn't keep the baby calves any longer than necessary though since they needed to be back with their mothers as soon as possible. Then they would be okay. They didn't have to fight siblings for food like the baby pigs did.

There was a year when I thought I was grown up and pretty smart (following my success with the lamb sales no doubt) when the "no Santa" rumor had caught my attention in grade school. But, just in case it wasn't true, and I knew a good thing when I had it, I continued to send my annual letter to the jolly old man at the North Pole. With the same good faith I had shown in previous years, I bounced out of bed on Christmas morning, ran down to the tree chuckling to myself about the cover-up I had so cleverly pulled, and ran over to my stocking that was hanging on the back of the chair. We had to hang them on the chair because we didn't have the traditional fireplace for him to plummet down. The stocking wasn't completely empty—it had the traditional orange—it was just that the toys were missing. But, there on the table by the chair where I always left cookies and milk, was my gift from Santa. It was a Bible. A small, black leather Bible of my very own.

It was a special gift with a very definite subliminal message directed to me: "It's time to grow up. We are wise to you." Well, it was worth the try.

Since we didn't have many choices, finding the right Christmas tree was an annual mission; we had to find just the right native cedar tree out in our pasture. Once satisfied with our choice, we sawed it down and got it set up in our living room usually using a five gallon can of sand to hold it upright. The aroma of freshly cut cedar filled our house. This was the start of our Christmas season so we were ready to start the decorating process. One year, though, we had our eye on a special pine tree in a roadside ditch not far from home. We carefully cut it down so we didn't break any of the beautiful branches, put it in our truck, and brought it home. We were so proud of that tree, but when we tried to take it in the house, it wouldn't fit. We had to saw about five feet off of our perfect tree to get it in through the kitchen door. We learned after that to select smaller trees because they looked a lot smaller out in the roadsides than they do when you get them in the house.

Decorating our tree took several days. We always strung popcorn to make ropes and sometimes we made paper chains out of colored construction paper. Christmas wasn't Christmas if we didn't make fudge the old fashioned way by beating and beating and beating (by hand of course) until it lost its gloss. Then it was ready to put into the pan to cool. Nearly everyone in the family took part in the beating process since by the time it was cool enough to put out in a dish it had required lots of hard stirring. We had to sample it to make sure it was perfect before letting it cool, then we would lick the pan clean to get every last bit. When it was my turn to stir I nearly always got my forefinger covered with chocolate so I could lick it clean once I passed it on to the next stirrer. We would make fudge other times in the winter, but it was the only candy we made other than at Christmas. We had our own walnut trees, so each fall we gathered the nuts, cured them, shelled off the heavy covering, then broke them apart to get out the nutmeat—another evening chore while we listened to the radio. The black walnuts made fudge especially good. Divinity was another Christmas candy we always made because it used the egg whites that were so plentiful, and again, our own black walnuts gave it that special flavor. Some years when we were really ambitious we had a taffy pull, which was a lot harder than stirring the fudge.

 Mom had a favorite Christmas poem that she would recite on Christmas Eve. It was about a Christmas mouse, and as much as she disliked mice, it was especially funny to hear her recite this poem. Since I enjoyed writing as well as reading poetry, I wrote a Christmas poem one year to include with my cards that was about a mouse that fooled Santa:

CHRISTMAS MOUSE

Once there was a tiny mouse
Who had no crashing pad and
It was getting nigh to Christmas—
Things were looking mighty bad.

PASSED THROUGH THE WINDOW ON MY WAY TO LIFE...

The little guy ran all about
Panic struck with fear
Darting in and out of every hole
To see if one was clear.

With the ground close to frozen
And the snow in line to fall
The cold and hungry gray mouse
Hadn't any luck at all.

But just as things could get no worse
He tried just one last ditch
Where other living guests before
Had opened up a nitch.

His eyes kept darting side to side
His nose was cold with fear
His ears set like two antennae
.In case that cat be near.

All was clear and looking good
As he made his merry way
To set up a little "mouse house"
Then, prepare himself to stay.

With hours of work so tiring
Gray mouse prepared to nap
With his little nest all cozy
His chore was now a wrap.

Suddenly, a great big thud!
He awoke from all the noise!
There by the chimney stood Santa Clause
With stockings all filled with toys.

Not one to miss this opportune
To check out what was new
And visit with that man in red
Gray mouse crept out to view.

"To beg your pardon, Santa,
That stocking's not full yet
I, myself can add one more thing
If you would like to make a bet."

At such a statement, Santa chuckled
And was quick to disagree
"This stocking can't hold one more thing—
It's as full as it can be."

Well, little gray mouse scampered up
Eager to prove his brag
And began to gnaw at the stocking toe
As if it were a rag.

When his chore was all completed
He scurried to Santa's knee
Smiled his little boastful smile
And stated (proud as he could be):

"If you will own dear Santa Clause
It did hold one thing more
As you can see that little hole
Was not in there before…"

There's a Time for Work and a Time for Play

One bright, sunny spring day, Dale came over for an afternoon of play and, since it was early spring and there wasn't much else to do, we set out to build a nest for the Easter Bunny. By the time we were done, we had built that bunny one long, continuous nest extending around the yard in all directions. Our yard was so large this nest was at least 100 ft. long end to end. I'm sure it would hold up in the Guinness World Records for Longest Easter Bunny Nest. The funny part was that by the time we raked up enough old grass for our project we had pretty well raked the entire yard for spring-cleaning. My folks must have had a big chuckle about that. Come to think of it, they probably planted the seed in my head and sat back to watch us work. Otherwise, had they asked us to rake the yard we no doubt would have complained about so much work.

During other times of the year Dale and I played in and on every piece of equipment and building we could find, from the highest top of the haymow in the barn to exploring the old abandoned basements of bygone buildings. The haymow was our favorite though because the loose hay made an excellent soft landing pad. We would climb up to the top of the haymow on ladders that were conveniently provided, then jump or swing on a rope down into the hay. Or, we might jump from the floor of the haymow down into grain that had been piled on the floor of the barn. If we did happen to get bored with that, we could always find something else to do. It's a wonder we didn't get hurt, but our parents didn't seem to worry about us—at least that we were aware of. One time I did step on a nail while playing (of course, I was barefoot) so I went out to the shed where my dad was working.

"I just stepped on a nail but it doesn't hurt," I told him, making sure he got the part about not hurting. Otherwise there may be a chance I would have to wear shoes after that. I scraped my feet and stepped on nails often without stopping play, but this time it was a major injury caused by jumping down onto the nail. Anyway, Dad got out a bottle of turpentine and poured it on the bottom of my foot, making sure it went into the hole so it burned good.

"That should take care of it," he said without any comments regarding shoes. Had it been my mother the reaction would have been different, but since Dad liked to go barefoot, too, he didn't comment. No thought was given about tetanus, even though we weren't ever vaccinated for it. The only vaccinations were for measles and smallpox, and it seemed like turpentine and iodine handled all injuries and open wounds. A neighbor did, however, put kerosene on his kids' hair after they came home with head lice. It killed the lice, along with much of their hair.

Playing on haystacks was the most fun of all, but it was kinda' hard on them. I don't know if the men appreciated us disturbing their neatly stacked hay, but they just couldn't be beat for fun. The work it took to get up to the top of that loose pile of hay or straw was enough to wear us out, but the fast trip back down made it all worthwhile. It was as safe a place to play as we could find on the farm.

When I was older, one of my friends and I mowed the grass into designs that spelled out each of our names. By the time we had our difficult pattern completed, the yard was mowed. I think that, too, was premeditated trickery on the part of my parents, but with the hours upon hours that I spent playing in our yard I guess it deserved some of my attention. It helped that by then we had a lawnmower with a motor on it at least. It wasn't a self-propelled mower, so we still had to push it, but it was much easier than the old reel-type mowers we had to use before. We had to take turns pushing those old reel-type mowers over the grass, pushing until we couldn't push any longer. Since I was so short I had an especially hard time. Lawns then weren't nearly as plush as they are now; the grass was thin and we certainly didn't put on any fertilizer to make it grow any heavier. Pushing those mowers about once a week was enough. We hand dug any thistles or dandelions that we found, and they were about the only two weeds we bothered with. At one time we got paid a penny a thistle for digging them out of our yard. Since I was barefoot so much, it was a benefit to me just to have the grass thistle-free anyway, but my sisters and I actually fought over thistles to get the pennies. Once we could use gas-powered mowers we began to take better care of the lawn to make it green and plush.

Our first such mower was built by Uncle Joe, of course. He simply added an old motor to our reel-type push mower. It worked perfectly until we actually purchased a manufactured one. He was usually a step ahead of the industry in his thinking. He did the same with our corn planters by fastening two of our two-row planters together to make a larger unit.

I would lay on the soft green grass for hours, especially on a nice, warm sunny day just watching the clouds move about creating designs of white and gray against the clear blue background of the sky. Sometimes they created an animal, other times a flower or a ship or a plane or anything my imagination could dream up. When the sun reflected against the edges it looked as if each cloud had a shiny satin lining attached.

I'm so thankful for my window. Thankful I can see families joining in the fun with their children playing games in the grass. I wonder if they realize what fun they are going to remember for a long time.

In the long summer evenings my sisters and I played anything from tag or hide and seek to just catching fire flies or simply running foot races (in our case, barefoot races). Dad loved to have us run races out in the yard. He would clock us to see who was the fastest, probably because I was much younger and would have never won a foot race with my older sisters had he not timed the event. He always gave us a fair start with, "one for the money, two for the show, three to get ready and four to (at that point he would hesitate a few seconds to catch any early starters) GO," then we would take off across the soft green grass with our bare feet flying just hoping to not step on a thistle that got by our yard maintenance work. When we caught fireflies we always put them in glass mason jars with lids shut tight, only the lids had holes punched in so the flies could stay alive. Sometimes we would pull off the body part that lit up, then rub it on our skin or put a chunk on our fingers—if we caught it just as it lit up bright, we had a shiny ring or bright mark on our skin for the rest of the evening.

It was a race to see which of us could locate the first star in the nighttime sky, then be the first to shout:

> *Star light, star bright*
> *First star I see tonight.*
> *I wish I may, I wish I might*
> *Get the wish I wish tonight.*

Then we would make our wish real fast thinking that the first one to do it would have their wish come true.

Along with running races and other games of competition, we would sometimes build our own high jump area with two kitchen chairs and a broom. Back-to-back chairs, wide enough apart to hold the broom, made an excellent makeshift high bar to jump over. It was more than high enough since we never did get to the point of clearing the top. Landing on the ground wasn't enough cushion, so we never wanted to try going over backwards or sideways to get more height. We jumped straight over and hoped not to fall or hit our shins on the broom handle. Again, since my legs were the shortest I couldn't compete with my sisters, but on the other hand, when I did fall it wasn't far to the ground.

Croquet was the most popular family game for us during the summer. We had a large, level yard that was ideal for setting the wickets a good distance apart. That just made it harder for me to compete, but with the mallets getting a little help from my feet, I tried to hold my own. At least they let me play croquet.

I hardly remember playing inside the house unless it was raining. Mom always told me to go outside and play to get the stink off. It was her way of getting me outside for some fresh air and out from under her feet. On rare occasions when weather did keep me inside, I liked to paint or draw or play board games—anything to fill the day—even sew cat clothing, but that's another story. In the cooler weather, I loved making (and eating) fudge and popping corn to pass away a snowy or rainy afternoon.

Television was unheard of, and the radio daytime shows were more for older folks, so I didn't bother to listen to those.

If a special day was in the near future, like Valentine's or May Day, I would spend hours preparing for those upcoming events. All valentines were homemade out of anything I could find around the house, but normally included construction paper, doilies and crepe paper. Then it was up to me to add buttons or lace or other sewing materials. Everyone I knew was included in my list: parents, school chums, classmates, teachers and I couldn't forget my uncle. One that I remember especially was for my parents when I was just learning to print. It was the typical red heart over a plain piece of white paper, then a white lacy doily was glued over the top of the heart with a red flower made of overlaying red crepe paper pieces. A penciled poem printed in my basic printing style read:

> *Who I am you should know*
> *But I send this sweet flower with the question Mother*
> *and*
> *Father mine*
> *Will you be my valentine?*

It was obvious that I wrote the words as they came into my head since they were randomly stuck in the lines wherever they happened to fit.

If the first day of May wasn't far off, I could always start getting my May baskets ready. They could be made out of about anything I could find; construction paper, some good glue, maybe small boxes or paper nut cups and anything else for decorations. Some spring flowers painted or colored on the paper completed that part, then at the last minute I would pick some live flowers out of our yard to add. During the spring I could always find violets; some years I would find tulips and white spirea. Once in a while there would be lilacs in bloom. If the year was too early (or late) for these flowers there were always yellow dandelions—they were no problem to find. The biggest part and most fun about May baskets was in the delivery. We would place them at the door of our friend's house on the evening of May 1st, knock hard on the door (there were no doorbells), then run away fast so they couldn't see us. We didn't include our name, so it was up to the wisdom or speed of the recipient to find out who had delivered the basket. When we went by car our parents would park down the road out of sight to make sure it was a surprise. Then after delivering the basket and pounding hard on the door, we would run as fast as we could back to the car for the getaway.

We could make our own paste out of flour and water when we had large projects like these. Normally there was a jar of store-purchased paste to use for smaller projects, but once in a while it would be gone so a backup plan had to be used. Our mother, being a former schoolteacher, knew about every way possible to handle emergency situations. Times such as this, it was handy to have her knowledge, but other times we didn't think so.

In the winter we played fox and geese, or sculptured snowmen, or occasionally we built a fort so we could throw snowballs at each other and then duck for cover. There never seemed to be any lack of snow. Snow angels were as close as we came to anything angelic. We went sledding nearly every afternoon and when the snow was really perfect we had sledding parties. When the moon was full, its reflection off of the white snow provided near daylight conditions. We would build a fire to keep warm and sometimes take food to cook, but we always had hot chocolate to drink. Snow was our winter entertainment, and we loved it, seldom giving it a negative thought. Perhaps the men in the family didn't appreciate it like we did, but I don't think they complained much. They knew it was a part of winter. Actually, it was a good part since it provided the moisture needed for crops the following spring.

During the next few years the polio epidemic hit hard and caught Dale. He was lucky to survive his illness with continued good health, but the scare of the deadly disease and the spread of infection was another whole new experience to the neighborhood. Since my mother had been inflicted with this terrible disease as a child, leaving her somewhat paralyzed, she was especially cautious. She constantly reminded me to wash my hands and make sure we took extra care with fly control. Dale and his family moved to a farm further away at about the same time our country school closed, and I was sent to town school so our time for play together became less frequent.

Even after losing my close playmate, I still had opportunities to play since my parents had friends come over frequently for a night of playing cards or just friendly conversation. One of my girlfriends and I became very good friends through this system. Since we did not attend the same country school, the only time we could play was during one of these visits; that is, unless we could convince our folks to let us stay overnight with each other.

Staying a night over at her place was a real refreshing time and I mean really refreshing. My room at home wasn't warm, but I did have a small amount of heat filter its way up the stairs. Not at her house—the only heat was what could passively saturate the floor from the living room directly below. Then the heating stove always went out during the night, eliminating that possibility. We had so many blankets on her bed we could hardly turn over, and to save our noses from frostbite, they too, were buried deep. In the mornings we were like bears coming out of hibernation in the spring. Once we hit the floor we made record times getting dressed to run downstairs to a warm room where the stove was. That warm-up time was brief before we had to head out back to the outdoor privy. Outdoor plumbing was just part of life for farm families so I was quite accustomed to that part of the visit. But oh, that freezing bedroom! I never could get acclimated to that. But as well as I knew how cold it would be there, I stayed over every chance I got. She was a friend, and it was worth every chattering tooth.

Birds of a Feather Flock Together

Our country school was three miles from home. It wasn't bad when I had a sister to walk with me, but when she went on to high school and I had to walk alone (since my ride on Silver wasn't very dependable) it wasn't much fun—in fact, sometimes it was even scary. Like the time when I was walking home from school and met a snake who was taking its share of the road right down the middle. I climbed over the fence into the cornfield and walked the rest of the way, scared to death. Never once did I think that there likely could be more snakes in the field than in the road. When I got home, of course, I was reminded of that. My mother especially laughed. She loved snakes. Well, I shouldn't say "loved" them, but she would pick them up in the yard and try to convince us how harmless the little creatures were. I never did buy it.

We had special games we liked to play during our recess and lunch times at country school. We had an hour for lunch, so if I ate fast I could play outside longer. My older sister, on the other hand, took the entire hour to eat her lunch. In fact, her teacher was known to have let her go to lunch early so she would get done before classes resumed. We were always told to chew each bite of food twenty times, and she was actually doing it! If it meant time away from play, I made sure my lunch went down in a hurry.

Auntie Over was a game we played nearly every day when the weather permitted. We had a small ball, softball, or whatever was available, then we divided into two groups—a group on each side of the schoolhouse. The object was to toss the ball up the roof on one side and let it roll over the peak and down the other side to the waiting opponents. We couldn't just throw the ball over the roof, it had to be rolled up and over. When we gave it a toss we would yell, "Auntie, over" so the kids on the other side knew it was on the way, but if it didn't make it all the way to the top (and about half of the time it didn't), we would have to yell out, "Pig tail" which meant that it was coming back down the same side. It was a funny game, but with all of the age differences in a one-room country school it was also one of the safer games for the younger kids to participate in without getting hurt.

Softball was a popular game if we could get enough kids in one place at one time to field a team. It only took a pitcher to throw the ball, a catcher to catch it, a couple of fielders, a batter and we had a game going. We had access to one ball and one bat that we all used no matter what size we were, but no softball gloves. We played it some at country school, but it wasn't very successful because of our age differences. The older kids got all of the hits.

Use Your Brain for Something Besides Holding Your Ears Apart

Since the bombing of Pearl Harbor was uppermost on my mind as I began my first days in country school, I tried to learn all about the war from my teacher and other students. We had weekly drills during those days when we would get under our desks for a few minutes to simulate an attack. I do know that when a plane flew overhead, everyone checked it closely to see if it had our star on the wing—an indication it was one of our planes. Since the planes didn't fly high or fast, the star was easily visible. Rationing hit our everyday lives since we had a hard time purchasing sugar, tires and gasoline. My sister was nearer the age of the soldiers fighting in the war so she wrote letters to them on a regular basis. In my aunt and uncle's family, four boys were in the war at the same time. These were trying times for them especially.

During these same wartime years, most of the high school girls had autograph books so friends could write them notes for posterity. Either they would make up something new or repeat what they had read in another book, but they were usually humorous. I think it was a way to connect with the war, yet help with the every day stress. Some of the more popular notes were:

When your work on earth is ended
And you're laid beneath the sod
May your name of gold be written
In the autograph of God.

I love you little
I love you big
I love you like a little pig.

When you get married and live by the river
I'll come to see you in my flivver.

Leaves may whither
Flowers may die
Friends may forget you but
Never will I.

Rose's are red
Pearl's are white
I saw them on the clothesline
Saturday night.

    Early one summer morning this same sister, who had just received her driver's permit, was driving over to pick up a neighbor boy to help with our haying. I was about six years old, and my big mistake, aside from riding along in the first place, was taking our new, young puppy for a ride. About half a mile from home my sister was looking at the puppy instead of the road and ran us right headfirst into the ditch. That was my first experience going in the ditch, and even though it was a very minor accident in a very small ditch, I would not ride in the car with her again for several months. In fact, I wouldn't ride with a woman driver for weeks after that—I rode only with my dad (or possibly another man driver). I was so mad at her. My lesson learned was to not take puppies along in the car, at least with a woman driver.

Dad couldn't say too much to her because earlier that year he had put our family car in the pond. We kids were skating out on our pond at the time when he decided he could drive the car out across the ice. When we suddenly heard a cracking noise, we got off as fast as we could, then we turned around to see him sitting in our car as it was dumped in the water. It wasn't in very deep, thankfully, because the ice was too thin to hold the car up long. But, we had to get a tractor and tow chain to pull it out. He had a hard time living that one down, but took it all in fun, actually enjoying the attention it caused.

"Miss Rae, how are we doing this evening? I see you didn't eat all of your dinner; didn't you like the potatoes? I brought you a magazine to look at this evening so I hope you enjoy looking through it."

Oh dear, I have a magazine to read. I wonder if my teacher is having me do a report on it because I'm not sure how well I can write. I just hope Miss Osburn doesn't read it in front of the whole school.

Teachers were good influences and I had many excellent ones— even piano teachers who, by the way, wasted a lot of their good time on me. One of my very favorite schoolteachers through my entire schooling was in country school. I attended kindergarten through fourth grade in country school, but I had her only during my first two years. I liked her partly because she was so young and pretty and partly because she seemed to understand that learning to read, write, spell and do math in front of a one-room school full of older students could at times be embarrassing.

My most memorable embarrassing wrong answer was when I answered Franklin Roosevelt was the first president of the United States. That pretty much brought the house (or school) down. Oh well, in my life, he *was* the first—that I could remember anyway.

Education came fast in the one room school, and faster during recess activities. When you are little and light as a feather, the teeter-totter is your worst enemy. After screaming from fright while held at the top cycle of this playtime monster, the question was always, "Do you want down?"

"Yes, yes, yes" was exactly what they wanted to hear, but entirely the wrong answer for my behalf. But, since I was caught in a very precarious situation for what seemed like hours, it had to be said. Before the last "yes" was out, I was the only one left on this monster machine as it came down—hard and fast—only to see the kids on the other end holding their sides with laughter. I didn't think it was very funny, but I had learned lesson number one in "teeter-totter schoolyard play." If you are the smallest, always be aware!

That's probably why I spent most of my time on the heavy iron (and conveniently round) rails that were on both sides of the porch entry. I was upside down, turning over and over on those rails so much that Dad finally built me some bars out on the playground. My legs, my knees, my ankles, my toes, one leg, one knee, my neck, my chin or any other body part that could support my weight were used for me to hang by. There were two bars, one higher than the other, so I had my own gymnastic Olympics right there. We could all be thankful there was no television at that time for any additional ideas related to uneven bars than the routines I had already visualized. With all of the upside-down playing that I did, my mother decided she should send a pair of slacks to school with me so I could put them on under my dress. Girls always wore dresses, so the question of "just slacks" wasn't even considered. There was of course the chant: "I see London, I see France, I see (whomever's) underpants." I'm sure I had that little ditty sung to me several times, but it didn't bother me any as I was only six or seven years old. I ignored them and figured they would get tired of singing it sooner if not later.

When recess breaks were over the teacher would call us all back inside by ringing the school bell, which was about the size of a small book. She would step outside on the porch and shake the bell hard back and forth in a rhythmic motion to make sure we all heard. If it was extremely cold weather she would just stick her head out the door to ring the bell. When the weather was that bad we weren't far from the door anyway. Sometimes in nice weather, my girlfriend and I would be playing in a small grove of trees in the furthest part of the yard, so it was good that she rang it long and loud. The grove of trees was fun, but none were large enough to climb or I'm sure that would have been my recess activity.

I never could understand why it was important for the teacher and everyone else in the schoolroom to know when we had to go to the bathroom. It wasn't only that we had to go, but by raising our hand with one finger or two fingers we designated the purpose for the visit. The only reason I could think of was to make sure we came back in the appropriate amount of time. The toilet was behind the school, probably a hundred feet or so. If we had held up one finger I'm assuming we should be back to the school room within a shorter amount of time than if we held up the two finger signal. One of the other students would have been sent out to look for us if we stayed out an excessively long time—we weren't about to have that embarrassment. It may have been a safety issue, although I never did hear of anyone falling in or losing their way.

For washing our hands, there was water in a bucket and a small wash pan on the bench. The water wasn't warm, but it served the purpose, besides we were used to washing with cold water at home. Each country school house had its own well close by with a hand pump so we could always have clean water to use.

After spending four years in country school as the only one in my class and the only young underclass person in the school, it was like Independence Day when a girl my age moved into our school district. Not only was she in my class, but we had the same first name. I couldn't have asked for more. Oh, did we have fun! She lived close to the school, but it was at least 1/8 of a mile to enjoy her company while walking home. And she was so funny. I had never met anyone with such humor. We went all through grade and high school together, but the most fun we had was back in our country school days; days when a few extra minutes to enjoy the snow or sunshine or a game of Auntie Over didn't spell out detention.

Students in country school

Music class was fun in a one-room country school since it included all of the students. We mostly sang in class, although once in a while we would form a band using a few simple, crude instruments. Our band was made up of a drummer, horn players, xylophone players, and other noise making apparatus. I played the drums. My grade school experience with band was much better than what my dad had when he played in the country school band, though.

During his school days the sessions were set so farm boys could, out of necessity, help at home. Because of this, some of the boys were pretty old by the time they got through grade school. Many did not go on to high school and very few went to college. Most farm boys could only attend the winter term which was for three months; early December to mid-March, during the time there was no field work at home. The other chores could all be done before and after school. In Dad's family, there were five out of the six kids in grade school with one other son in college all at the same time.

Dad's favorite teacher

Our music classes included singing at least one patriotic song. Other songs varied, recognizing every nationality, race and religion that made up our young country. "My Old Kentucky Home," "Old Black Joe," "Dixie Land," "Bonnie Laddie," "Old Folks at Home," "The Little Brown Church," and "Carry Me Back to Old Virginny." We also had religious hymns such as "Silent Night," "A Hymn of Thanks," "Mother's Prayer," and of course many patriotic songs. One of my favorite songs, "A Frog He Would A'wooing Go" was a long song with thirteen verses. The first verse was about the frog who went a'wooing, then followed his experience down to the last verse: "The Frog and Mouse they went to France, and that is the end of my romance."

We especially liked singing rounds to "Row, Row, Row Your Boat." "She'll be Comin' Round the Mountain When She Comes," "You Are My Sunshine," "Playmates," and upbeat music such as these three were popular as well.

Our teachers arrived early during the winter months to start the coal stove—in really cold weather we could sit around the stove until the room got warm enough for us to go to our individual desks. Wet mittens and overshoes were placed around the stove to dry before the next recess or our trip home.

Each desk had an attached seat sized to fit the student. It also had an ink well and a place for pencils along the top edge. Tops on some desks could be raised to make storage areas for books, tablets, rulers, crayons and other necessities, but normally there was simply an opening underneath.

When necessary, teachers boarded with farm families in the neighborhood. Our school had a few who did, but the two teachers I had were married to nearby farmers so they could drive to school each day.

After she graduated, Mom taught high school in one of the small towns. Then after she married my dad she didn't teach anymore other than trying to teach us kids at home. From rhymes to grammar rules, we heard all of the teaching tools that she had used on her pupils. "Ain't fell in a bucket of paint" was one reminder, and when I would say "me and Dale" she would immediately ask me, "Oh, is Dale mean?" So, we were well aware of how school children were taught by the time we went to school. We grew up hearing her favorite sayings all intended to be an educational message. Obviously, she had a saying to fit every situation and she didn't hesitate to use them. I knew immediately what she was trying to impress upon me in her wily way with some of them, but others I didn't have any idea what they meant or where she came up with them. There were terms such as "chewing the fat," "upper crust," "saved by the bell," "dirt poor," "puppy love," "it's raining cats and dogs" and especially, "Don't throw the baby out with the bath water." Where did she ever come up with that one, and what could such an obnoxious thing mean? I never did bother to ask since most of it just passed right on over my head. I hoped I wouldn't hear them again—that's probably what she meant by "in one ear and out the other."

Dad was strict with our grammar, only not in the same sense. "Darned" was about as close to swearing as we were allowed, and even that made him frown. If we happened to slip up and say

"Danged," which was pretty popular slang in those days, we were threatened with soap in the mouth. It didn't sound like anything I wanted to risk, so I watched my slang language pretty close, especially when my parents were nearby.

Beauty Is Only Skin Deep

Box suppers at the local schoolhouse were an entertaining food feast. They were called box suppers because all of the ladies (yes, even we younger ones) would very artistically decorate the outside of a cardboard box, many times an old shoebox. On the inside we put our prepared meal for two. Most of the time the meal would be specially prepared chicken, some side dishes and, of course, a very special pie. Men in attendance would then bid on the unmarked box that appealed to him most, not knowing who had prepared the special one he had his eye on or what was inside. We would often see men smelling the boxes trying to decide what was inside so they knew which one they wanted to purchase. The money taken in at box suppers was used for schoolhouse upkeep as well as for books and supplies. Once he confirmed his purchase by yelling out the highest bid, the preparer would go over to thank him. After all the boxes were sold, everyone ate, visited and enjoyed the evening. I was always afraid some "old" man I didn't know would buy my box, then I would have to sit with him during the meal.

These suppers usually brought in enough money to purchase needed items for the school since they were so well attended. Sometimes a program followed the meal, sometimes card games, and other times just relaxed conversation.

Early to Bed, Early to Rise, Makes a Man Healthy, Wealthy and Wise

When our small country school closed and we were consolidated with the school in town, we rode the school bus about nine miles. It was unbelievably convenient compared to our previous transportation, which was mostly by foot. Riding a school bus was a new adventure for me, though. I usually spent most of my time arguing with somebody—much of the time about cars or tractors. I think the only two (at least very well known) automakers at that time were Ford and Chevy. My family always drove Chevys, so I had many hot debates regarding that controversy. Nobody could ever convince me that Chevys weren't the best, because my dad said they were. They probably just did it to torment me and hear me argue, but if they did, it worked.

One of my good friends and I played "Peas Porridge Hot" to pass the travel time, so we got to the point where we could whip through the motions to that with exceptional speed. It provided entertainment during our ride home, plus it no doubt helped with my basketball dexterity as I got older.

The bus stopped right at the end of our yard. I could just run out the door, jump off the porch, run across the yard and hop on the bus. Nothing could have been more convenient. I did fall when I jumped off of the porch one morning, turned my ankle and went down to the ground with a thud. When I tried to get up and continue my run out to the bus, my right ankle wouldn't support any weight. One of the knights in shining armor saw my predicament and came to my rescue by helping me hobble my way on out to the bus. Since my first morning class was geometry, taught by our basketball coach no less, I tried to hide my noticeable limp. When he called on me to go up to the blackboard for a problem, the secret was out. He muttered something I couldn't quite understand, along with a low-pitched grumble, and immediately took me to his office for an ankle taping and a pretty hefty lecture to go along with it. I loved to play basketball, so from then on my ankle was taped before every game—in fact, both ankles were taped as a precaution. I was also a bit more careful when I jumped from the porch after that.

Many times when I had overslept, my mother would hand me an egg sandwich as I ran past her on my way out the door. It was my breakfast the fast food way.

Basketball practices were held the last period of the day unless we had a game scheduled. Practices were scheduled like that so we could be dressed and ready to catch our buses back home at the 4:00 p.m. bell. School hours were from 9:00 a.m. to 4:00 p.m. It was a full day.

To help me get in physical shape for the approaching basketball season, I would ask the school bus driver to let me off a couple of miles from my home so I could run that distance. The driver thought I was out of my mind, but I enjoyed the run, plus I knew it would save some tough conditioning later. By then I knew enough to stay on the road even if I did see a snake—I just shared the road with the snake, only I ran faster.

I was fortunate to suit up for a few high school basketball games when I was in 8th grade. Wouldn't you know, a member of the opposing team hit me in the right eye during my first two minutes of the very first game. Our coach put a patch over it for the night with orders for me to see the doctor the next day. Our local doctor said it was a scratched cornea, put a black patch over my eye and ordered me to wear it during the daylight hours. I looked like a pirate for a week.

Our basketball uniforms were satin, so they had to be washed and ironed before every game. As our student manager, one of my very good friends was responsible for all of this pre-game preparation, plus she kept all of our supplies readily available in case of any injury. With two games scheduled each week and more often than that during tournaments, it kept her pretty busy.

The first time I got to wear real basketball uniforms was for junior high games. Our team was so excited to actually have uniforms we didn't care that they were the old hand-me-downs from the previous high school girls. They really were pretty cute even though some fit and some didn't. They were short white skirts, pleated in the front and back. No underpants were attached to the skirts so we wore a couple pairs of our regular white cotton pants under them. A previous high school team went to the state tournament one year so the wife of the coach handmade all of their uniforms, which were these same suits. They well could have been the first satin uniforms worn by a team in addition to being short skirts. They were a long way from the long, black cotton leggings which were typically worn at one time.

Better Safe Than Sorry

In college I played some basketball on the intramural team. Since it was just pretty much for entertainment, it wasn't all that exciting. There was also an interpretive dance club. Now this was a lot more fun, especially with so many good friends involved. I didn't have any background or lessons in dance, but I caught on pretty quickly, and since I was so limber (thanks to my grandma) it was easy for me. When there was a need for a limber dancer, I was available. It was easy for me to bend over backwards, put my legs behind my head and do all sorts of twisted contortions. My mother always told me when I was younger that I would get stuck that way. She also told me that if I stuck my tongue out at anyone, it would get stuck that way, but since that didn't prove to be true, I didn't pay any attention to her about the contortions either.

We were required to take physical education classes in college just as we had been in grade school. The difference was that in the grade classes in our small town, everything was geared toward basketball. During the winter months we had tournaments among teams representing different grades, and this was the highlight of the year. High school kids refereed the games, so that was almost as much fun as playing even though most of us weren't very good at it. At the conclusion of the tournament there would be a grade school tournament champion crowned. You would think the higher grades were always favored, but many years the younger grades such as fifth or sixth grade would end up the champions, much to the chagrin of the older kids.

Our high school senior class was small (actually twelve in all) so we were very close, and since we were all from farm backgrounds, we had a lot in common. When it came time for us to plan our senior trip, which was a common practice for each graduating class, we were refused permission by the board of education. Since we had worked hard all through high school to earn the money needed for our trip, we were not only disappointed, we were mad.

With the help of our superintendent, we took our trip to Chicago by leaving the same night AFTER we all graduated. We had a bus waiting outside for us to board as soon as the ceremonies were over. It was a lot of fun with a lot of memories, none the least was doing something we wanted to do without the board's approval. I guess our superintendent wasn't your normal school administrator. He taught classes along with his other duties, and it was usually off the subject matter. So much so that I don't remember what class he taught, but I do know he had us bring an invention to class for our homework. There were several excellent ideas, from farm gates to peach pickers, which was mine. I used an old coffee can with a small feed sack fastened to it, with the entire picker part fastened to the end of a long pole. The idea was to reach up into the tree and hit the peach with the edge of the coffee can so it would gently drop down into the sack without getting bruised. All of the ideas were farm related, either work saving or safety devices. Our class was pretty inventive as was obvious by our senior trip solution.

After graduation and our trip were over, I moved into town to be close to my work. I didn't have a car so it was important to live near the city bus line. That was my transportation to and from work for a year. Since I didn't know where I wanted to work and didn't know what was available, I applied at a small clothing store for a sales position. Wouldn't you know it, they hired me to be a sales associate in the lingerie department. I had been a tomboy all my life, and now I was going to sell lingerie! What irony. Actually, I only worked there long enough to find a secretarial job with a large insurance company. I was a little more suited to that position. I worked there a year before going on to college. The extra money was nice to have, although my parents would have paid for my college expenses had I asked them. I just liked to have my own money. In fact, during college I worked at the local lumber yard or any other work that was available. Pay was terrible. I think from twenty-five cents to fifty cents an hour. College town; lots of cheap labor.

College certainly was not all work though. I had my share of fun—probably more than my share. I made so many lasting friendships and joined in on any activity I could find. When I could find the time, I fit in some class work. Going from a small high school to a small college wasn't a big change for me other than the larger variety of subjects. My favorite classes other than physical education were the sewing and cooking classes, so I spent most of my effort on those.

Physical education in college was more about exercising routines—more stretching, sit-ups and things of that type rather than basketball. Most of the girls hated it, but I thought it was fun—it was my favorite class in college. One day our teacher had the entire group of girls (probably twenty or more) stand on one leg with our other leg bent at the knee raised off the floor. She had us put our hands on our hips, close our eyes and see how long we could stand upright balanced on one leg, stork style. I stood there for what seemed like forever, but with my eyes closed I didn't have any idea who was left standing. So I waited and waited with my eyes still closed. I don't know if it was my basketball experience, tree climbing, or playing in the haymow, but I had an exceptional sense of balance. Eventually she just blew the whistle for us to stop because I had been the only one left standing for so long that she was afraid I was going to stand right on through the next class.

One of my new friends was an exchange student from Costa Rica. Since she taught Spanish as a night course, I took the class. It didn't last long enough to really learn a lot of Spanish, but I caught on to the basics and had a lot of fun trying. She was so much fun to be with, everyone loved her.

I was invited to visit the sororities on campus to meet the girls and see what sorority life was about. My first impression at each open house was that they all smoked. Since my experience with smoking as a young child had left me sputtering and choking, I declined joining a sorority, but instead joined a club called the Independent Club. That seemed to fit my style more. The first Homecoming, as a freshman, I was invited to ride on our float with one of the senior girls pretty exciting for a young, green, freshman girl.

We had dances and parties just like the fraternities and sororities, but probably a little more subdued. For our part in the annual Homecoming program, we each danced to a song of a different era in time. My dance was the Charleston, which was the first era—naturally I had no idea how. It was actually pretty much fun once I caught onto it. I could see why my mother liked it when she was in school, but she thought it was pretty funny to see me try it.

Use Your Head, Not Your Hands

In our consolidated town school we played softball every recess, lunchtime and any other time we could get outside to the high school baseball field since that's the only place we had to play. There were lots of kids available now, all close to the same age, so the equality made it more fun than trying to play with the older kids like we had experienced in country school. The only bad part here was that the boys were so much better since they all played baseball. As a result, most of us girls were timid—I was not good at all and pretty much content to stay out in the field and just let the ball drop on the ground. Because we always played work-up, I didn't have any choice; eventually I was forced to bat.

When our recess started the work-up team fielded itself by whoever ran out to the field first (knocking down anyone in their way) getting the choice position, then so on down the line as we arrived. The last one there was right fielder, which was usually me. Not for long, because the player starting in right field soon went to center field, then left, then into the infield with third, short, second, first, pitcher, catcher, and then bat—in my case it was soon back out to right field, then to start all over again. I always hoped that I didn't make it all the way up to batter before our recess time was over. Our rookie style of play drew a lot of teasing from the boys, but since girls' softball wasn't an organized sport at that time we didn't get the practice the boys did playing baseball. I could normally hit the ball, it just didn't go far enough for me to run anywhere.

Amazingly, after I was out of high school I did play softball on the town team one summer. And, we actually wore gloves—that was a whole new experience for me, but it was a great hand saver. A high school baseball player was nice enough to let me borrow his baseball glove. The lady that formed the team played on a professional women's softball team, so she was an excellent coach as well as player. Maybe that's why I was much better then, but still nothing to brag about. At least we were playing against other women and not the men's baseball team. That certainly helped.

During my high school years, I wore blue jeans at least two times each week. I would say I was on the edge of fashion, but since jeans weren't popular then, it would have been the bottom edge. In fact, the only jeans I could find to buy were boys' jeans since girls' jeans weren't available. On occasion, I would wear my western boots along with my jeans. It may have been for the comfort or it may just have been to be different or make some type of statement, I really don't know. Since I had always been the tomboy, jeans and boots were just part of my normal wardrobe. It's only fitting that my favorite song was "Ragtime Cowboy Joe," and my wardrobe fit my musical preference. You would think that the music I sang in public would be country music, but it wasn't. Had I been able to sing my preference it would have been, but my vocal teacher didn't allow it. She always had me sing classical music—I think because it took more practice, more lung capacity, and required staying on key. She didn't much like country music.

Once in a great while I would drive the family car to high school, but not many kids did. If they lived in town, they walked—those who lived in the country rode the bus; this dictated that all extracurricular activities be scheduled around bus boarding times. When we got into our regular basketball season and had to catch the game bus, our parents would take us in to town, or we would just stay there after school until time to board the game bus. To save a trip, staying in town was the most normal pattern, then after the game our parents would meet us back at the school to take us home.

On one special tournament day we all had our pre-game meal at a team member's home in town before we left for the game. Her mother fixed us a great meal with lots of high-energy food for our upcoming game. I believe our coach actually told her what to prepare. One other time we ate at our school before leaving for the tournament game. Two of the senior team members fixed the meal, and I will never forget the Jell-o. It apparently hadn't been mixed well and turned out like thick, sweet rubber we were supposed to eat.

We were nearly always rewarded for winning a tournament by stopping after the game for a victory meal. Since there were no fast food places, we stopped at real restaurants for big sit down meals. On very special occasions the restaurant owner would treat us to the meal free, if not, the coach or some of the parents made certain our meal was paid for.

My parents drove to nearly every game, so it was easy for them to know when the game bus was back in town. My dad loved to watch me play basketball. He was so very proud of my talent, however he still laid out the rules. Rule No. 1: First and foremost there would be no crying on my part before, during or after a game no matter what the reason, particularly for fouling out of a game. No tears. He always said that I would not play any more basketball if I did. I took him at his word, although I'm not sure which of us would have suffered the most. Since I fouled out of a majority of the games, I had many opportunities to put it to a test, with probably the biggest test coming when our team was within a point or two of going to the state tournament. But, I never did take that chance and never did shed a tear, at least that anyone (other than my pillow) could see. I don't know why he was so strict about that with me—he didn't make the same rule for my sisters. For some reason he just wanted me to be tougher; he wanted me to be more like the men in the family.

During the first two years of high school and one year of junior high, I was a cheerleader for the boys' games. After our game was over, I would run down to our locker room, shower, of course, and get that tape off of my ankles. Then I would change into my cheerleading uniform and be back up to the gymnasium in time for the following game. There apparently was no limit to my energy level. That's probably why I could eat like a man but weigh only a little on the high side of a hundred pounds.

Oh how I would love to have some of that energy level now. I would go home and see Silver again to make sure he is okay.

Make Hay While the Sun Shines

They haven't brought me my dinner yet. But it doesn't matter; I'm not really hungry. It would be so much better to be eating at home. Why do I need to be here in this strange place anyway? I wonder what they will be eating tonight and I wonder what the conversation will be. I miss them so much already. I suppose they are talking about the crops and the weather, and maybe a little politics. Whatever, it would be so much nicer than the loneliness of this dreary room. Try as I might, I just can't remember why they thought this is the best place for me to live. I didn't do anything wrong that I know of. Plus, the dingy gray paint on these walls is so drab it doesn't make me feel any better. I'm not going to complain, but it just isn't what I like. I would prefer a brighter and more cheery color like red or bright pink—anything but this gray. It really doesn't do anything to improve my appetite either even if dinner was here.

One time at home we painted the upstairs hallway while our mom was away. She had wanted it painted but had to go to the hospital for surgery before it got done (and when she had some input). Well, with all good intentions, and not much good decorating skill, we painted it as a surprise for her when she returned home. It was a surprise all right, since we had painted it flamingo pink. She was pretty much speechless. That is probably a good thing, since we later realized what she really thought about it but didn't want to tell us. She even left it that ghastly pink long enough as to not hurt our feelings before painting over it. When she finally did paint, it took three coats of paint to get rid of that bright pink and back to the light beige she had originally wanted. I'm sure that pink paint is still under there somewhere.

My two sisters and I were so busy trying to get the work done while she was in the hospital it gave us a good idea of how much work she did each day. We tried to cook—that was a time when our dad's Army cooking experience came in handy—and keep the house clean, the clothes "warshed" (we, especially Uncle Joe, seemed to insert an "r" in many words) and ironed, and the furniture dusted. It was during the summer months so at least we didn't have school work to include in our list of duties. Neither did we have the semi-annual cleaning to do either. When we had spring and fall cleaning, it was so intense. All of the large room rugs had to be hung out on the clothes line and beat hard for several minutes to remove the dust, the beds had to be completely taken apart and cleaned, with the mattresses aired outside in the fresh air and sunshine, and of course beaten with that same metal rug beater. The floors that were exposed around the outside of the room rugs were cleaned and waxed, the curtains were washed, or in the case of heavy drapes, taken down and hung on the clothesline to freshen in the breeze. All of the windows had to be washed inside and outside, all of the kitchen cabinets were emptied and washed, and every few years they had to be painted as well. Some of the bedrooms had clothes closets and some didn't. Those closets had to be cleaned each season with the out-of-season clothes packed away until they were needed again. Thankfully during this time our mom was away, we girls were just trying to keep up with the daily cooking and cleaning. That alone was more than enough for us.

Dusting the furniture, however, was a chore we were quite familiar with through our normal weekly duties. Dust cloths were recycled underwear, the ones that were too thin to wear and had the elastic all stretched out. Rayon underpants made excellent dust cloths after being treated with some type of liquid dust control. Once dry, they were good for a couple of weeks, then we put them in the wash to use again. It helped to have four females in the family to furnish our old, worn-out undies. Some items like the dust control liquid could be purchased from a route salesman who made rounds throughout the countryside selling his products. He usually came around about four times a year with everything from cleaning supplies to medical and cooking supplies. The cooking supplies were things such as vanilla and food seasonings while the medical supplies were mostly medicinal salves or ointments.

Make Do With What You Have

The aprons my mother always wore would be an improvement over what I see these nurses wearing. At least her aprons had some color. I wonder where I put my sewing machine. I think it's here in the closet where my blue dress is hanging; maybe I can get it out and sew something more attractive. I know they would like that.

I always wondered why mother wore those big aprons that were almost a dress without sleeves. After I thought about it, I realized no other piece of clothing had so many uses. Since I was a very shy child, I distinctly recall hiding behind my mother and pulling that apron out in front of my face thinking I was completely hid. It also served as a handkerchief when Mom's nose was running. In fact, it served as a handkerchief when my nose was running since there were no such things as tissues in a box, and it sure beat rubbing my nose on old newspapers or catalogue pages.

The aprons were made in a variety of styles to suit the owner, but all of them covered her entire dress, always had large pockets, and they all tied in the back. I imagine it saved dresses from getting dirty for at least two days. It was better to put on an apron each morning, since washing and ironing those was much easier and quicker than dresses would be. I don't ever remember my mother wearing anything other than print cotton dresses with the printed cotton apron over them, unless she was going down to the river to go fishing. In that case she would wear a pair of my dad's overalls. With all of the outdoor work she had to do, and in all kinds of weather be it hot or cold, rain or snow, you would think it more comfortable to wear something warmer. Of course, long cotton stockings were the necessary vogue during cold winter weather to keep her legs warm— especially since nylon stockings weren't available yet. When nylons did begin to surface, the wartime rations pretty well kept them out of sight for several years. Anyway, the cotton ones were heavier and much, much warmer for winter wear.

Those large aprons also served as a wash cloth since my face was nearly always dirty from playing outside. That was disgusting to my mother, but all she had to do after catching me was dampen the corner of her apron and clean my face with it. What a versatile tool. She dried her hands on the bottom part, used the top part for holding sewing and mending pins, and it worked in a pinch for holding hot skillet handles or those slippery mixing bowls when stirring bread dough or cakes. It couldn't be beat for wiping away the tears when one of us would get hurt or upset, either. The apron bottom even made a quick basket replacement for picking up a few eggs when Mom needed some to make dinner. We normally gathered eggs in a bucket each evening, but when she needed just a few she pulled up the corners of her apron, gathering them in one hand so she could pick up the eggs with her other hand. Of course, not only eggs, but a small amount of garden produce fit perfectly in that little apron pouch.

When did the full apron fade away to be replaced with a half apron? Why did they fade away anyway? They were a necessity! I think it was during the late 1940s or early 1950s. Was it because the automatic washer became popular? Was it because there was no need to clean chickens several times a week? Or, was it because we kids were growing up and didn't need the sniffles wiped from our noses or the wet end of her apron to wipe the dirt off our faces. I don't know. I do know that it valiantly filled its need during those years of service.

Iron skillets were almost as much of a necessity as the full aprons.

It seems everything we ate was somehow prepared in our large iron skillet. For breakfast we used it to fry bacon and eggs, then at lunchtime it was the chicken or the steak or the pork, then during the evening meal (which we always called "supper") it was used for the fried potatoes or whatever main dish we had. There were leftover potatoes from our dinner most of the time; if they were mashed we mixed some eggs in the leftovers, made patties out of them, and fried them in the skillet. Oatmeal (Dad had it every day) had to be cooked in a pan, though. It was one of those pans we disliked washing, especially if it got dry. My mom always preached to us, "Put cold water in the oatmeal pan as soon as it's empty. It will wash out easier." And you know she was right, but nine times out of ten we would let it set (more procrastination) until it got really dry. Then we would complain. My biggest request when it was my turn for dishwashing was to let the pans set overnight in the sink since I didn't like scrubbing the gunk out. Not only out of the pan, but out of the sink strainer when I got done washing the dishes. I never did get my way ab that et it either. No matter how bad the pans were, they had to be cleaned after each meal.

    Sewing new aprons out of inexpensive fabrics or cotton bags was almost as common as making quilts. Of course, they were both a little above my sewing expertise, but I was always around to watch the action when the ladies of the church got together for an afternoon of hand quilting. Our dining table was large enough to hold the quilting frame, so as many as seven or eight women could sit around it, each working on their own section of the quilt. Every quilt was unique since each was constructed of fabric scraps donated from various families. Some of the better quilters made small stitches that were even in size—some of the newer quilters hadn't perfected it yet so their stitches were large and uneven. I didn't let any scraps of fabric go to waste either. With a treadle sewing machine (one without electricity so it had to be pumped with our feet to make it run), I learned fairly young how to use up any small scraps of fabric by making garments for every cat on the farm. Those poor cats had to put up with me dressing them and undressing them for hours at a time. They were much more of a challenge than dolls since cats were moving models. It taught me to design, plus sew with pretty good accuracy. Once the electric sewing machine came about things moved along much faster. I'm sure it was a nightmare for my mother since it was easier for me to hit my fingers with the needle, plus it did a lot more damage when I did. It happened a few times, but I was persistent.

You Can Do Anything You Put Your Mind To

This self-taught sewing program has stayed with me throughout my life. All of my young daughter's dresses, as well as most of my own, I handmade. I did make some shirts for my son, but I don't think he was very fond of them. In the beginning I didn't have a sewing machine of my own so I borrowed my mother's. Determined to get my own machine, but without enough money to buy one, I started trying to win a free one at the state fair. It just so happened that the fair had a category for homemade articles made out of feed sacks. It was a big challenge I was going to undertake—the construction of cat clothing in my past would be put to a test. Many things other than chicken feed came in those large cloth sacks so I had these available. We used so much flour and sugar and, since we didn't get to the grocery store that often, we purchased flour and sugar in one hundred pound bags, so I also had those to use. The feed we purchased for the baby chickens was actually the best source for pretty cotton bags though. Most of the time our sacks were made into towels for drying dishes or aprons for Mom, or cut into smaller pieces for quilts, but I did find a few I thought appropriate for my new project. Since there were specific category requirements that had to be met, the selection of each cotton bag was important. To win the sewing machine I would need to receive the most first place ribbons in this division.

Once the classes were released I began to sew an article for each class which ranged from men's shirts to quilts to toys to dresses and other various categories. After entering each item at the fair, I couldn't wait to see if I won. As soon as I thought the judging was completed, I ran down to see the results. Well, I was disappointed that first year; I received one first place ribbon—not enough to win the machine. I was second though, and there would be another year to try again. As soon as the fair was over I again started collecting cotton bags in preparation for the next contest. When the categories were made public, I continued searching for that perfect bag for each class. I was on a mission. I selected each bag for the best possible pattern for use to make each item. I made an adorable little baby crib quilt with little hand embroidered animals on each block. I made matching mother/daughter dresses. I made a western shirt with hand embroidery on the yolk, and a swimsuit with a cute little cover-up and matching bonnet for my baby daughter. I made some place mats out of some of the really heavy bags by drawing yarn through the edges. The most fun was making the toys; these were made out of some gingham-looking sacks and some calico-looking sacks. Of course, they were the gingham dog and the calico cat. They were unique. In fact, they were on the cover of the weekly statewide newspaper as one of my blue ribbons that, yes, won me the sewing machine. I was so thrilled. I used my new machine constantly from then on, returning my mother's machine back to her. Of all categories I had three first places and four second places. It was so much fun and such a feeling of satisfaction and accomplishment.

Gingham Dog and Calico Cat

Monkey See, Monkey Do

Everything appears to have an acronym these days, so I will have to say while growing up on the farm I was a "PTK,"or "Pre-Television Kid." Most everything I can remember while very young was on the radio. All of the old radio shows, mostly the comedy shows, stand out in my mind, like Gracie Allen and Red Skeleton. Those comedy shows were popular, but an interrupted news report about the bombing of Pearl Harbor was the most memorable. When I heard that Pearl Harbor had been bombed and not knowing what that meant or even what destruction a bomb could do, I ran into the kitchen to find out; "What happened, what happened?" I quizzed, but got a very brief and vague answer. I could tell by the news reports that it was important, but my parents didn't want to upset me. It was obvious to them I was concerned, but they thought I was too young to worry. They were careful to eliminate undue stress while we were young to just let us enjoy being kids. This war thing, though, was something different and it didn't go away. After several months of hearing reports on the news and seeing the front pages of the newspapers, it was hard to keep worry away. I became interested in what was going on, what was happening to our soldiers, and how our leaders were helping end the war. Even though my parents didn't think I was paying attention, I was. One day I drew a picture on my tablet paper of a desk with an empty chair and footprints leading out through the open door. Under the picture I had written, "She's gone again" referring to Eleanor Roosevelt. My dad had a big laugh and kept it in his war scrapbook for a long time. What ever made me think that the wife of a president could help win a war by staying at her desk was a puzzle. Apparently I thought women were an important part of our country's security if they just stayed home where they belonged, and apparently I thought she wasn't fulfilling that obligation. What a thought.

My first experience with television was when the owner of our local appliance shop brought a TV set over to the high school study hall one day so we could watch a World Series game. That was one time everyone wanted to stay in study hall because we got to actually watch Bob Feller (our hometown baseball player) pitch for the Cleveland Indians that day. Of course, once I saw it, like every other student there, I was hooked.

Not long after that, I convinced my dad to go watch this new invention at the shop in town. I was sure it would show him just how much we, too, needed one of those picture tubes in our home. Of course, he got hooked too, never a doubt. He was hooked on the *Dinah Shore Show*. We got one television for our home, black and white, but that did it! As soon as I got home from school I would turn on the TV. It didn't make my mother very happy when she caught me wasting my time watching "that show." That show she was referring to, of all things, was a space show, *Captain Video*.

As a rule, our television did not get turned on until after our evening meal and we had cleaned up the dishes and swept up the floor. For cleanup, we each had our tasks that rotated—one for washing dishes, one for drying, and one for clean up. Only then could we turn on the television to watch evening programs. It started to vary a little when the news came on during the six o'clock hour—then my dad would sneak into our living room to watch the news while the rest of us cleaned the kitchen.

I played a lot of games as a PTK since it was possible to listen to radio shows and still be able to concentrate on checkers or caroms or cards. We played a lot of caroms since Dad was so good. Once any of us got good enough to beat him, we didn't play caroms as much anymore.

We played a lot of cards too, a lot of games—anything to fill the evening hours before we went to bed. Television put an end to that; like other families, we sat around and watched television unless we had set a special night to play cards or games. I gotta say, pre-television was a lot more family fun. Not yet being adept at sitting around doing nothing but watch TV, I still couldn't do it. I was usually upside down in the chair or on the floor—my feet on the back and my head on the seat.

Every so often, for what reason I have no idea, unless he thought we were all catching a cold, Dad would get out a can of juice (usually orange) and personally serve each of us a large helping. We were pretty much required to drink it if he served it. Of course, it wasn't as good as fresh oranges or juice we prepare now, but it did have the essential vitamins we needed during cold winter months. The prepared fruit juice came in large half gallon cans and was usually grapefruit or orange juice or pineapple juice, but we seldom bought that. It seemed to be a big thing for him to serve us all juice, so everyone drank up.

When I was very young Dad taught me his favorite hat trick, then he would be so proud when I showed off my new talent to our visitors. It was like the shell game only using baseball caps. Instead of beans, I used small pieces of newspaper, wadded up as tight as I could get them, then to get them really tight I put them in my mouth to soak. The trick was that there were nine of these little, wet balls of paper and three hats. I could pick up the wet balls between my fingers (even my small fingers) hide them under the hats so nobody could see what I was doing. Then by simply pounding under the card table with one hand I could make the balls jump from one hat to the other. It was amazing. The amazing part was that everyone acted like they didn't catch on. Dad and I thought it was a big deal anyway. As the youngest in the family, apparently it was up to me to provide the entertainment.

One of my other entertaining acts I performed was antics to the "Monkey Song":

We went to the animal fair. The birds and the beasts were there. The old raccoon, by the light of the moon, was combing his auburn hair. The monkey he got drunk—sat on the elephant's trunk. The elephant sneezed and fell to his knees, and that was the end of the "monk."

And then there was the popular and much in demand performance to:

I'm a little tea pot, short and stout
Here is my handle, here is my spout
When I get all steamed up then I shout
Tip me over and pour me out.

    It took plenty of room for me to perform my "shows," so it was important for our living room to be large. Large enough to accommodate all of the actions I could think up anyway. This was probably better than television anyway—a precursor to the *Ed Sullivan Show* no doubt.

    We used the card table almost every night for something when we were PTK—if not cards, then some type of table game. One of the most bizarre things we used it for was what we called "Table Up." Two of us sat on opposite sides of the table with the palms of our hands placed down very lightly on the table. As we all sat around the table chanting "table up" constantly, the table began to rise off of the floor. Once that happened, we would begin asking questions that it answered by the number of taps it made on the floor. This was almost spooky during the actual rising part. Usually when we got to more personal questions we helped the table a little too much with the answers. About then we all got mad, and the game ended until we decided to try it again some other night.

    My first experience with a major fire came when I was out in our yard watching off in the distance as a neighbor's corncrib burned. Even though it was over four miles away, the bright fire lit the darkening evening sky across the valley. There was a lot of nervous excitement, with many questions on my part, as well as a subterranean fear. I ran around the yard watching the bright orange light over the hill, yelling to everyone within reach of my screaming voice and to every car that drove by our yard on the way to see what was happening, "Helliker's corncrib!" trying to share my newfound discovery before they found out for themselves. It didn't enter my mind that I had their name all wrong by saying it backwards, but that fire made a lasting awareness of fire destruction and danger.

    I have always been a weather-watcher. I learned that from my dad as well. He kept a scrapbook of all prior weather records back as many years as he had access to them. My mother, of course, thought this was silly. She was more of the thought that if it rains, it rains, and if it doesn't, it doesn't. Anyway, I always went with him to check on the rainfall after each rain. He would roll up his pant legs, take off his shoes and go barefoot—since I was always barefoot anyway, we would walk out in the muddy fields together checking for moisture in the ground, the black mud squishing up between our toes as we walked.

    I guess it was only natural that many years later when the county needed a weather watcher for the U.S. Weather Bureau they called on me. I actually think somebody donated my name. Anyway I was the official weather watcher. During that time I thankfully had no tornadoes to report. Since I was always watching the weather anyway it made sense for me to watch for everyone else as well. We lived up on a high ridge so I had a good view of storms coming up across the valley from the west.

    Dad always went out in the yard to check the western sky and see if we were going to get rain, then be ecstatic if we did, particularly if we were in a dry spell at the time. With no radar available to predict the weather a day in advance, the western sky was about as good at predicting rain as we had available. There were also the old wives tales about raining when the crickets did this or when the locusts did that, but those were pretty much guesses. When it rained hard our entire family would pile in the car and drive down to the river just to see how high the water was getting and how fast the river was rising. This was my opportunity to drive our car by sitting on my dad's lap.

I did that from the time I was old enough to hang onto the steering wheel, but of course my legs were only long enough to reach the seat from my squatting position. Since we seldom met anyone else on the road it was pretty safe. If we did happen to meet another car, Dad took over the wheel.

Both my dad and mother grew up living by the river so they both knew what devastation it could cause after exceptionally heavy rains. Dad called it "on the warpath." It was normal for the river to get out of its banks when on the warpath, then once it got to that stage it wasn't much longer before it crept out over the road. We were warned to never drive in the water since it had a lot of power as it rolled out across the road. Once in a while Dad would drive in it just a little way but never when the current was swift. One of the neighbor boys had his car pulled over to the ditch by the water current one time and was fortunate to get out of his car before it was pulled into the river.

Driving down to check on the river was just that much more fun since we always drove by what we called the "little store," and with enough persuasion (I don't think it took a lot), we would stop. This store was one small room out in the country, but it had all of the good stuff like candy and ice cream. It also had staples such as bread and small sacks of sugar and flour—the types of things that could get us by until we got into the larger grocery store on the weekend. We always had a good visit with the owners of the store as well as other neighbors who were out checking on the river or just stopping by. It was a great little store.

Once I got old enough to actually drive a car, and my legs were long enough to reach the floor, I begged to drive every chance I could get. Dad wouldn't let me drive alone though, then he made the mistake of telling me when I could change a tire by myself I could drive by myself. With that promise it wasn't but a few days until he came home from town to find a new tire on his car. He also kept his promise.

One year (I think I must have been fifteen) Dad got in the car to go somewhere. As usual I jumped in to tag along with him—it didn't matter where he was going. Once we got to the river, he got out and walked for what seemed like hours. He crossed over the river and back again several times on downed tree logs with me right behind him. We ended up several miles from where we left the car. I'm not sure what prompted that hike in the woods, unless he just wanted to relive his youth on the river. I do know he was deep in thought, hardly speaking a word the entire way, in fact he hardly checked to see if I made it across the logs. He probably knew he would hear a big splash if I fell in, but it was all I could do to keep up with him and still stay on the dry side.

Share and Share Alike

There were always card parties between neighbors and friends each year. These were great fun because, unless we were old enough to stay home alone, everyone got to go to the party. What else could they do with us kids? Babysitters were unheard of. While the adults played cards, we would find entertainment elsewhere in the house—usually an empty bedroom. Once in a while, we would check in on the adults to see which couple was winning and which couple was losing. The hosts always gave the high-scoring person a nice gift, with a "booby" prize gift for the sorry individual having the lowest score. The booby prize winner was of course teased from then until the next party when they could try to redeem themselves. There would always be at least four tables set up – normally it was five or six.

Card parties were held in the winter months when farmers weren't busy working in the fields, so it seemed we always had high snowdrifts to drive through. The roads weren't nearly as wide then, and it didn't take much for the snow to completely fill the ditches then quickly move on across the roads, especially if there was a brisk wind. But, it took a really bad storm to cancel a card party. There was never anything like pop or tea to drink, however the hostess always served good food, like sandwiches, desert and coffee.

I'm not sure what we kids did to entertain ourselves for the night—probably some kind of trouble. Normally we would get sleepy long before the party was over so we either had to wake up and walk or be carried out to the car for the trip home. Since I liked to be carried, I could fake a pretty good sleep. Most of the couples lived within nine or ten miles of each other, yet it seemed like we were driving to and from the next state. I always thought it was kinda fun to sneak a peak at the opposing players' cards and try to help my dad out a little by telling him what cards they were holding. That usually got me a big boot out of there and back to playing with the kids. The card games weren't anything fancy—just plain old seven-point pitch. Tables would be all over the house; usually one group at the kitchen table, then maybe one in the bedroom, and more in the living room. The losing partners would change each game, so if you had a really good partner you tried hard to keep them. There would be one head table, and high scorers gradually moved up to it or, if you were a losing couple, you moved back down. A set number of games were established at the beginning of each party so couples remaining at the head table were considered the winners when that final number was reached.

It was late summer, after the crops were all in the ground and after the haying and threshing was all done, before there were any summer get-togethers. They would be held more during August or September. At these neighborhood parties, homemade ice cream, pie and probably lemonade would be available. Fewer neighbors came to summer events—these were more like neighborly visits.

Idle Hands Are the Devil's Workshop

Like all farm families, my parents put in long days involving lots of hard work. They were always up early to begin the day, but the field workday always ended at 5:00 in the evening to allow time for chores. Chores were usually done by 6:00 so we could eat supper at exactly that hour, then the rest of the evening was spent relaxing, playing games or going for a visit. After the noon meal (12:00 on the dot), my dad would usually sit down and rest until 1:00, then go back out to work. Uncle Joe would always lay down on the floor to take his after-dinner nap, his head propped up against the corner of the doorway. When he got up he would have a deep crease in the back of his head. It was all that much more obvious since he had no hair to hide it. It seemed important for them to keep this schedule. I'm assuming this is what they were taught out of necessity when electricity wasn't available. Likewise, no fieldwork was done on Sundays, only the care of our animals.

Of course, there was no such thing as a microwave oven. The closest thing to it was an electric toaster. Tanks of gas used for our cooking stove sat alongside the house as close to the kitchen as possible. Copper tubing ran through the wall so it could be attached directly to the stove. Replacement tanks were delivered routinely unless we ran out early, then we either had to go pick one up or have it delivered ahead of schedule. Years later we had a large tank that held one thousand gallons of propane gas so we could use it for not only cooking but heating the house and later even heating our water.

Prior to using oil or propane, our house was heated with coal that we hauled out from town in our truck, then unloaded into our basement. It was scooped into a coal chute that ran down from a small window in the basement foundation, and placed so the coal ended up in a large pile on the basement floor. The coal pile was kept close to the furnace—a huge convenience when it came time to shovel coal into the furnace.

One Halloween when I was in grade school, probably about second grade, we had a school party that required wearing a costume. Since we always had plenty of coal available, my sisters decided to cover me with coal dust—all of my exposed body parts. They actually rubbed that stuff all over me, including my face, so I definitely was disguised. They had way too much fun doing it, and I sure didn't see either of them putting coal dust on their faces. I learned why later that night. After all of the fun came the realization (particularly to me) that this stuff wouldn't come off. We used every type of soap and oil we could think of trying to get me clean. That part of the costume negated all of the fun I had at the party. I'm sure the devastation to my skin stayed permanently.

When we updated to our oil stove, it was placed in the dining room, yet furnished heat for the entire house. A house that was a two story with eight rooms, four up and four down, was a good-sized area for one stove. It was a labor saver, however, since the oil was piped into the stove and the men didn't have to shovel coal any longer. We had one open register between the lower and upper floor that allowed some heat to rise upstairs. It never did get toasty warm in our bedrooms. On really cold days we would all go sit by the stove with our feet as close as we dared without burning them. On exceptionally cold nights our mother would heat some water in the teakettle, put it in a fruit jar and seal it with a good rubber ring and mason lid so it didn't leak, then let us take that to bed. It was not only warm on our feet, but helped distribute some warmth throughout the bed as well. It's amazing how close the rest of our bodies could get to our feet. We looked like large balls rolled up around a fruit jar with nothing sticking out from under the covers.

Several years later when we did get our propane furnace that actually blew warm air throughout the house, it was like heaven. There were still no registers in the bedrooms, but we had the benefit of a little heat rising up from the lower level; enough to make winters more bearable. About the same time, we installed indoor plumbing so about then we thought life was getting pretty soft.

Man Works From Sun to Sun, but Women's Work Is Never Done

Cooking for the threshing crew was the biggest cooking event of the summer for farm wives. The farmers in the neighborhood went from farm to farm working as a crew to get their oat or wheat harvesting done. My parents owned a threshing machine—one of the few in the neighborhood—so it was used by all of the neighbors. Only when they came to our farm was I allowed to participate. I looked forward to those three or four days when the crew would be at our farm, but it also meant that I had to help prepare the dinner each of those days. Since our dining room table was very large when stretched out to its full length, all of the men could sit and eat at one time. There would be twelve or fifteen men all with huge appetites come in from the hot fields. Of course, the house wasn't cool either, but we did have fans running once we had electricity. The meals were always enormous. It would take all morning to prepare the meal, every detail starting from scratch. We cooked fried chicken, roast beef, noodles, mashed potatoes and gravy, vegetables and about every kind of homemade pie for desert.

Sometimes there was additional help. Many times Ruth would come over to help us prepare dinner. Chickens were killed and dressed that morning. My mother could kill chickens with a lot of speed, even with her handicap. It's kind of bad to think about now, but at that time it, too, was a fact of life. When the baby chickens we had either hatched at home or purchased earlier in the year weighed about three pounds, we could start butchering them for fried chicken. The chicken's heads were removed by a variety of acts depending on a person's favorite method, then the rest immediately dunked in a vat of scalding water. This steaming hot water loosened the feathers enough so that by quickly pulling and rubbing at the same time most of the main feathers were removed. This was another art that showed off the skill and practice of farm women. To singe off any remaining feathers, Mom would light a tightly rolled-up newspaper and quickly move the flames all over the bird before the paper completely burned up. Once this was done, I was always appointed the "inspector" to go over the chickens a final time, removing any small pin feathers that remained. I took great pride in my work since they bragged about how good I was with my "keen" eyesight. Once the chickens passed my final inspection we took them into the house where Mom would cut them up into the serving pieces. That, as well, was so routine for her that she did it with ease and speed, plus with her doing it, all of the parts were as they should be. Not in my case, however. I never did get the hang of it so I stayed with the feather project.

It remains all too clear in my mind that we helpers couldn't eat until the men were done and out the door. That was so hard to do when we had worked all morning preparing this huge meal. To smell the food during the time they were eating and we were waiting just made our appetites increase. By the time we could eat we probably ate as much as the men did. It was a good thing, because we had all of those dirty dishes and pans to wash and dry when we got done. I was especially anxious to get that over with so I could get back outside and watch the threshing take place.

Before the men came into the house to eat, they washed off the sticky chaff and dirt they had picked up while working out in the hot field. We had a bench (the one we used to put the separator on while we washed it) out in the yard with a pan for water, a bar of soap, and a towel. We sat the bench over close to our well so they could easily hand pump enough water for washing. Even though the water wasn't hot, it felt good to get that dirty chaff and dust washed off. There was no indoor plumbing, so apparently that part was taken care of before they came in for lunch. After eating, everyone went back to the field with a very full stomach, usually rubbing it with both hands and thanking my mother for the delicious meal. That helped make up for her hard work since she was proud of her accomplishment. I didn't care about the pride end of it, it was what I wanted to hear because then I knew I could eat.

One year during threshing time we took the crew into town for their meal at the café. My mother had just been released from the hospital following surgery and didn't have the strength for the hard work of preparing such a large meal. And for some reason (probably to stop my whining), I got to tag along. Boy was it a big deal for me going along with the threshing crew. Plus, eating at a café just wasn't something I had been involved in much before that day. No doubt it was a good meal, but nothing like my mother would have prepared.

Having extra people for meals wasn't that unusual, but having that many hungry men at one time happened only at harvest. Otherwise my uncle, along with the five of us, was there every day for meals so Mom was used to cooking large meals.

We had our own homemade butter when I was very young, but later we started using butter from the creamery. The creamery truck came by on its route, picked up our whole milk, and then brought us butter when it came back around the next trip. We did keep our own separated cream from our morning milking to use.

As for our noon meal (dinner), we always had meat, potatoes, bread, butter, salads and always something sweet (usually pie). My dad's favorite was lemon pie, so we had it often, especially before his diabetes was diagnosed. Since I was always starving before dinner, I had a habit of eating food out of the pan before it was cooked, especially raw potatoes. As Mom peeled them and put them in the pan to cook, I would take them out to eat. I loved them raw, and she didn't seem to mind me eating them—apparently they had some nutrition value, plus we had plenty either out in the garden or stored in the basement. When I got old enough, she made me peel my own potatoes.

Much of the raw food I ate, other than vegetables, contained raw eggs that are now considered a health risk because of possible food poisoning. It didn't seem to cause us any problems. Every time there was a bowl used for cookie dough or pie filling or cake batter or frosting it was a skirmish to see who could get to it first. With cookie dough, the bowl didn't even have to be empty. We seldom had anything left, but when Mom made frosting for cakes she usually made an extra large amount. Then we spread the excess on graham crackers—this served as fake cookies in an emergency when we couldn't find any real cookies. When we got home from school, like most kids, snacks were the first thing we looked for as we came in the door. In a rare case of not finding anything already prepared we made do with some of our own concoctions. It may be bread and butter with sugar sprinkled on top, or it may be raw oatmeal with butter and brown sugar mixed together. A precursor to granola, I guess.

We butchered our own animals for meat—a hog or two several times a year; but one steer would last several months. This meat, plus our chickens, provided our entire meat supply. I wasn't excited when we butchered 'cause that meant we would have the "odd parts" to eat, like liver, heart and feet. It is true—we ate everything but the "squeal" when we butchered hogs. Our meat had to be canned until we had access to the locker in town. We canned so many fruits and vegetables even after we started taking meat to the locker that we still had six large shelves filled with canned items. Each day I would bring several jars of food up out of the basement, and after each evening meal the clean jars had to be taken back down to the shelves. It was done every day, too—they were never left for the following day. With all of the produce we canned and kept in the basement, it was a constant turnover of full and empty jars. Between taking jars down, bringing food up, taking clothes upstairs, and bringing dirty clothes downstairs I often felt like I was constantly running up or down the stairs. Especially since I was the youngest and "fleetest of foot" as Dad called me, I was the one they always counted on for these errand-running projects—just another one of those perks for being the youngest.

After we butchered we made laundry soap out of the rendered lard. Rendering was done by cooking meat scraps over a very low heat so it didn't burn, or worse yet, catch on fire. Some of this liquid fat was then used to make soap by mixing in lye and sometimes a bluing agent for extra white clothes. Once the soap was cooled in the containers and became solid again, we sliced it into bars for washing clothes. Lard was good for cooking as well, and actually the only thing we used for baking pie crusts. When Mom fried steak in the iron skillet, she always put some of the fat trimmings in to cook first before adding the meat so it didn't stick to the bottom of the pan. We had steak often, especially round steak. Since round steak isn't a tender cut of beef she would put it on the cutting board and, with a large, sharp knife, pound and pound on it until it was porous and limp. I was usually involved with that pounding project—it would have been a good way to take out any aggressions if I had any, but at that age I didn't know about such things. Then, she dipped the steak in flour, added salt and pepper, and it was ready to fry. Once it was cooked, the browning in the pan bottom made delicious gravy. I loved the gravy and usually ate any that was left after our meal was over. I would even eat the liver gravy but try as I might, I could not force myself to eat the liver.

Summers were one continuous canning season. Without any type of air conditioning, and with the stove in constant use for not only food preparation but canning, the kitchen had to have been hot all summer long. It's funny though, I don't ever remember complaining about the heat. It may have been because the doors and windows provided cross ventilation, or it may have been the heavily shaded yard or that we were simply acclimated to it.

At bedtime it could be pretty unbearable though. Since the windows on the upper level were close to the floor, my sisters and I would find the window with the most air movement and sleep on the floor as close to the window as possible.

Most meals were large since there were always six of us at the table. And all meals were at the table. During the winter months our evening meals weren't anything special; we might have soup of some kind like potato, vegetable, oyster (once in a while), chili or what we called "spectus" which was nothing more than cooking a crumbled egg/flour mixture then adding milk. We had boiled eggs, cornmeal mush, rice, or some form of potato most nights. We would have the leftovers from our mush supper the next evening, only fried with butter and syrup. We had pancakes or waffles along with some of our home produced sage-seasoned sausage fairly often during the winter. There were four sage bushes in our garden so each fall we pulled off the leaves to sun dry so we could keep them available for seasoning the remainder of the year.

With everything being made from scratch, at times we had flour all over the kitchen counters, noodles drying over the chair backs before being cut into strips and pans of bread dough on the table. We had a flour bin that held 100 pounds—that's how much we used. It seemed like we were always cleaning up flour, plus everything else it took to prepare so many meals. With such a plentiful supply of chickens and eggs, we had chicken and noodles at least twice a month when it was time to use the older chickens for food. The noodles were made with the yolk part of the egg so there were lots of egg whites left over. The best and fastest way to use up extra egg whites was to make angel food cakes. My mother made so many cakes she didn't need or use a recipe—she could tell when the batter was just right. She actually was so experienced that any time a judging contest was held she easily won. Actually, I make it sound too easy—it wasn't. Every farm wife made lots of angel food cakes for the same reasons, but it seemed Mom had the technique. The old pan she used was so old and dull it appeared to have been passed down from my grandmother. For some reason I could use that same old pan, same ingredients, and what I thought was the same technique, but my cakes never turned out as light and fluffy.

Flies were always a problem. With so many animals out around the barn, it was normal to have some flies make their way to the house. Using a newspaper rolled up to form a swatter, we guarded the kitchen doorway while people went in and out. Again, this was a chore for us kids. Just inside the back door where the flies loved to congregate, long sticky rolls of flypaper hung from the ceiling. These fly traps were about two feet long after we pulled them out of their cardboard packaging, and they were completely covered with an exceptionally gummy substance. If any flies got past the doorkeeper or if they just snuck in some other way, they were doomed by the sticky paper. Not many survived past our porch area to make their way into the kitchen.

To protect his ankles my dad always wore high top shoes, always black, and laced up in front. He wore them everywhere. He never wore bib overalls, but many farmers did and swore to their comfort. Even though his ankle tight shoes kept the dirt out, he always managed to get his pant leg cuffs full of whatever he happen to be working with that day. But, as his mother had taught him, before coming into the house he would reach down with both hands and briskly slap both sides of his turned down pant leg cuffs until they were clean enough to roll back up.

Early morning chores included getting the cows milked before breakfast. Once the milking was done and separated (the process of dividing the milk from the cream), the separator was brought up to the yard and placed on a wooden bench to be washed. Until electricity became available we had to turn the separator handle by hand. To wash the separator we carried hot water from the kitchen stove outside to the bench, then again for the final hot water rinsing. It was a daily chore that had to be done soon after breakfast, and before we started preparation for dinner.

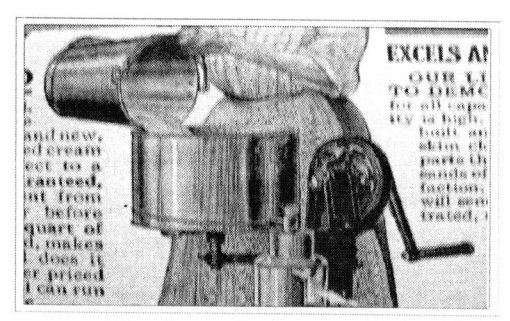

Hand-cranked seperator

Our cows were kept up by the barns overnight then let out to pasture after we milked. When it was time for the evening milking chores we would either walk or ride the horse down to bring them back in from the pasture. Milking, of course, was done by hand—we didn't have that many cows, but normally about ten. I was pretty good at milking. It wasn't something I was required to do in the mornings, but usually I would take my turn for evening chores. If we had a crippled cow or an older cow I would get to milk her. Sometimes the cows would be a little ornery and be known to kick; we had metal "kickers" to use on those cows. Kickers were steel forms that fit over the cows' hocks, then connect by an adjustable chain to fit different sized cows. Our milking stools were little wooden benches made in the shape of a "T" so we could sit on the top and balance ourselves on the one leg. I think this was so we could stay nimble and get out of the way in a hurry if need be.

Our many cats stayed out around the barn to drink the leftover separated milk, but our dogs stayed around the house to clean up kitchen scraps. They were our only available garbage disposal. Prepared dog or cat food was unheard of I assume, at least we had never heard of it. Had it been available, we wouldn't have wasted the money to purchase it. Our cats were valuable for keeping the mouse and rat population down, and our dogs helped some with herding the cows, but their primary purpose was as companions. I don't know if they would have saved us in a life threatening event or not—thankfully they weren't tested on that—but it's pretty doubtful. Plus, their cattle herding ability was usually to our detriment. The very first dog I remember having was a white, medium size, short-haired dog that I called "Sport"; he was old at that time. After he died, I convinced my parents to get a puppy that was more of a collie type. Even though he looked like Lassie, I named him "Bingo." I don't think puppies were very favorable to my parents because of their care and mischief, but, of course, I promised to take care of him. Bingo was also the puppy that caused our "car meets ditch" problem when my sister was driving.

Our dogs did warn us when predators or unexpected people were near, but not enough to keep the Halloween pranksters from playing tricks on us. The boys in the neighborhood loved to upset outhouses, let out livestock, upset wagons, move gates from one place to another, and any other mischief they could cause. My dad actually got a kick out of it and looked forward to the next morning when he could check out what pranks they had pulled overnight. When some of the boys would cut through the yard on their way to more mischief, he would hold the flashlight beam across the grass just high enough to keep them staying low. He thought it pretty funny to see how long they would lay flat in the grass. If the grass happened to be wet it was just that much more fun. Dad was a kid at heart. I didn't get involved in many pranks until I was older, but since there wasn't such a thing as "Trick or Treat," our only alternative was that of a prankster. The closest I came was breaking up a watermelon patch one time—I think the melons were too old to eat anyway, but we though it was, oh, so risky. The grounds at the high school always received the worst tricks—it seemed to be the prime target every year. Most years the boys would turn a goat or pig or some other animal loose on the property. I think everyone just expected it so there were no county marshals on duty to keep everything shut down and the kids out of trouble. It was Halloween—it was expected.

After the evening milking we didn't use the separator since we kept it as whole, rich milk. Pure cream from the separated morning milk was used in everything from coffee and cereal to homemade butter. The separated milk was too weak for drinking—at least in those days. It was more like skimmed milk, so we made cottage cheese out of some and fed the rest to the cats. By letting the milk sour and curdle, slowly cooking it and then straining off the liquid, we had perfect old-fashioned cottage cheese. Churning butter was sort of fun, watching it go from cream to butter, but we didn't make it as much after we started getting butter from the creamery. The liquid drained from the butter was good buttermilk, if you liked buttermilk.

Mondays were always wash days. It was a hard and fast rule. The first washing machine I remember using was still a ringer washer, only electric. Thankfully I wasn't involved in hand washing—the hand-cranked separator was enough. Our washing process started by using extremely hot water we had heated on the kitchen stove. We used this for the first load that was the white linens and bedding. Then the next load was colored nice things, then colored dirty work clothes, then the very last load to run through were the small rugs. This was all done with that one load of water. The washer had a pretty nasty agitation to it so you sure wanted to keep you hands away. After the clothes were agitated for a while, depending on how dirty they were, we would put them through the ringer to get the soap out. We were even more cautious to keep our hands out of the ringer since it could grab your hand along with the wash. As they came out the other side of the wringer they fell into a square metal tub of hot rinse water. Using a heavy wood stick, rinsing was done by swishing the wash around in the hot water, then putting them back through the ringer, only this time they dropped into a basket to carry out to the clothes line. Clothes baskets were made out of the wood fruit baskets we had lined with an oilcloth fabric to keep the wood dry. Imagine the savings of water and soap using this system. Apparently the soap was strong because even with everything going through that one load of water the wash was always spotlessly clean. The lye probably had something to do with it.

We carried the baskets of clean clothes out to our backyard clothesline so we could hang them up to dry. Once in a great while in some of the very coldest weather we would hang lines up in the house but Mom much preferred they dry outside. Lines could be hung from the door transoms going from door to door throughout the kitchen so we could get at least a couple of lines up. Mom usually requested that we hang them outside even in freezing temperatures. They actually froze dry and would be so stiff we had to bend them over to fit in the baskets. Of course our hands also got pretty well frozen along with the clothes so it didn't take us long to make the trip. We made record times pulling off the clothes pins and the frozen wash, tossing everything in the basket and running back into the house. That was one step. Next, dry clothes were sprinkled with water, tightly rolled up, and placed back in the basket to wait for ironing the next day. My mother was good at dipping her hands in a pan of warm water and whipping the water onto the clothes in smooth, even strokes. It was her experience that made her so good, I guess, but she could sure go through a lot of clothes in short order. Later, we used empty catsup bottles with a bottle stopper in the top. It made sprinkling a lot easier for us inexperienced in the hand whipping style since the stoppers had holes evenly placed around their tops.

The next day, Tuesday, everything was ready to be ironed, and pretty much everything was ironed with the exception of bedding and wash towels. Any articles that had holes or rips were kept for mending on Wednesday, and everything else was put away. Mom didn't do a lot of sock mending, or "darning," as it was called, but many farm wives did.

While I was very young, in fact before I was old enough to use them, the irons were put on the stove to heat. We used two sets so when one flat iron got too cool to use there was another one ready. The main part of this system had a wooden handle with clamps to hold the hot iron bottoms. It wasn't long before we had electric irons—by then I was old enough to get in on the duties.

You Can't Teach an Old Dog New Tricks

The only place I get to see candles anymore is in the banquet room. I can't go down there often, but I like to see the glowing candlelight on the tables. One night when the lights went out in my room I was allowed to have a candle for a short time. I was so sad when they took it away.

When electricity came to rural Iowa it changed the entire rural scene. Oil lamps that previously hung on the walls were replaced with electric light fixtures hanging in the middle of the rooms. During that same time, our rural community gained access to telephones for a whopping $3.75 for three months use. The phones also hung on the wall, at first, until they were replaced with dial phones. The wall phones had to be hand cranked, which was a bit tricky for me so I wasn't allowed to use them. Each party on the line (I believe we had 10) had a different number of rings including some short, some long, and some a combination of the two. Getting through to the operator so she could place a call was no problem since it was one long ring. If we would have had an emergency I could ring her without any problem. Of course when anyone's phone rang, everyone on the line knew who was getting a call, and many times everyone on the party line would listen in. Not that everyone was nosy (although we had a few of those, too), but the calls were so infrequent that neighbors feared it was an emergency they should know about. When phones were first installed it was a unique thing for farmers since they were used to having complete privacy. One family, in fact, answered the phone by saying "Beamans be not at home." They thought it would keep callers from knowing they were home, not realizing it actually was just the opposite. That was one of the funny things my parents would laugh about.

By the time Monday, Tuesday and Wednesday were over most of the timely, weekly work was done unless we had canning or extra baking to do. Thursdays were often filled with something for the church; either the church ladies would get together and quilt on that day, or they may meet for an event planning session.

There were different ways of making money for our church expenses. The Ladies Aide Society worked several different ways, such as meals that could be anything from soup suppers to chicken and noodle or meatloaf suppers, or any other variety of meals. Each fall they held a harvest sale when the fruits of their labors were sold. It was a time to sell the beautiful quilts, hand-embroidered dish towels, hand-crocheted items, rag rugs, or any variety of other handmade articles. One project was a collection of recipes from each of the members. These books were very popular so they continued to bring in funds for several years. One of our favorite ones was for corn bread. We had it to eat each time we had bean soup and ham hocks.

> *Corn Bread.*—Heat one quart of milk; when it boils pour it over one good pint of corn meal, in which one tablespoonful of butter has been mixed. Stir till the batter is quite smooth, then add four eggs beaten very lightly, the yolks and whites separately, stirring them in while the batter is hot, and bake it at *once*. Speed is everything in making this cake successfully.

Corn bread recipe

A Watched Pot Never Boils

Time came when we could buy factory made bread, but not only that, it was delivered right to our door. A driver brought bread, rolls and even sweets out to our area on his weekly route. We thought we were living the good life to have these available without having to bake. The side benefits to buying our bread were the wrappers. It didn't take long for homemakers to find uses for those plastic bread wrappers, even though they weren't completely air tight. We used them for everything—then we washed them out, dried them, and used them over again. These useful little bags were the only things we could leave laying on the kitchen counter after we washed the dishes. That was so they could air-dry overnight. There were no "Ziploc" bags or anything of that convenience, but a small rubber band served as a pretty good substitute.

Chickens were not only a mainstay for our food, but they were relatively easy to care for. They mostly required a watchful eye while they were babies, so farm wives and kids handled those chores. We always bought our baby chickens in early spring before fieldwork began so the men could help out with heavier chores, mainly cleaning and bedding the floors in preparation for their arrival. Unlike other animals, baby chickens can begin eating dry food as soon as they hatch out of the shell, so our small feeders were filled with finely ground grain their tiny beaks could pick up. Because the weather was still cold, small little brooder houses were used to keep them warm. Our brooder houses looked like tents with heating elements attached to the underside. Between those warm tents and nice warm bedding, the baby chickens had no problems keeping warm—that is, unless the electricity happened to go off. When that happened, as it often did in rural areas, it was a panic to keep the baby chickens warm and alive until the heat resumed. Since chickens grow relatively fast they would be heavy enough for us to start eating after a few months. I didn't mind them as babies—in fact, they were fuzzy, cute little yellow things and fun to play with—but I immensely disliked the old hens. If I hadn't been persuaded in a most forceful way to gather eggs, I would have completely avoided it. The hens scared me to death when I had to reach under them to take their eggs away. It seems like they knew I was afraid because they always pecked my hand—everyone else in our family seemed to get by without any retaliation on their part, but not me.

My sister and I had more arguments over that chore than any other chore we had to do, even dishes. In fact it was during one of those heated arguments over who's turn it was to gather the eggs that caused our dad to step into the picture with an iron fist. That's the only time I remember being hit with anything other than a flat hand (or that old razor strap on my rear parts), but it did stop our arguments. Since he seldom became involved, apparently our mother had called him in for reinforcement.

At any time of year we had either young chickens to eat fried or the older hens to use in scalloped chicken after their egg production dropped. Since we had so many chickens of all ages, we always had plenty of eggs available. When it got to the point where we had more than we could use in everything we could possibly think of, we sold the extras. We had a pretty reliable car by then so we could take the eggs to town when we went in for groceries on Saturday evenings. The eggs paid for our groceries with maybe a little money left over. We thought groceries were expensive compared to prices in my grandparents' day. They purchased mostly the same items, including the Post Toasties cereal, which was not exactly considered a staple item, for a mere twenty-five cents a box.

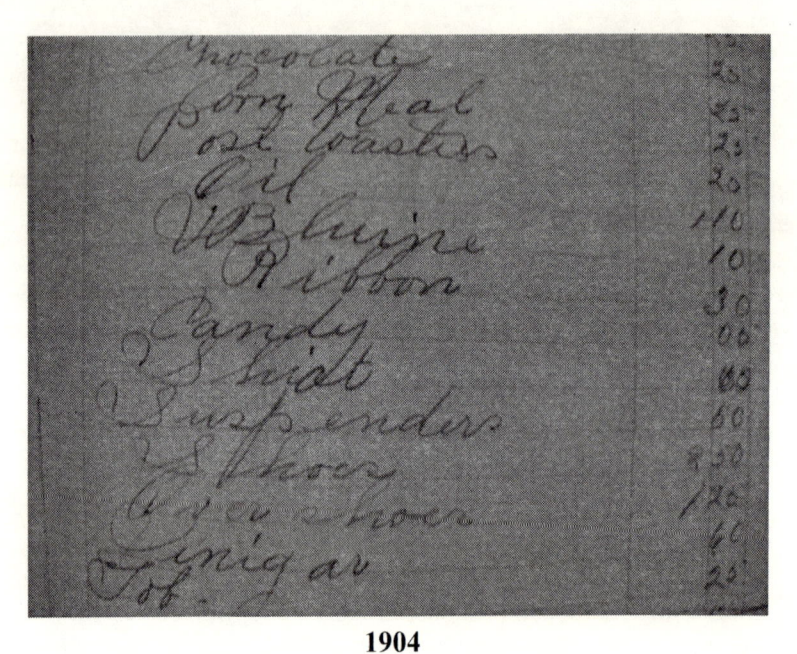

1904
Grocery entry in ledger

Waste Not, Want Not

The nurse told me we are having ice cream for lunch today. I hope it is homemade. That would be so nice since I'm very hungry, and we haven't had homemade ice cream since I came here to visit.

Eggnog was one of those egg-based foods that was a cure for every illness. It was made with raw eggs, beaten to a thick, creamy substance, then good whole milk was added, a little vanilla for flavor and we had the ultimate cure-all treat. At this stage it was much like homemade ice cream except not frozen. Homemade ice cream was made more often during the summer months, but we had it for special occasions all throughout the year. In the winter we usually made it to take someplace like to church suppers or school functions. Since the milk and eggs were so plentiful all we had to buy was some ice in the summer—in the winter we could just chop ice out of the tank or pond. When we did buy ice we went to the nearby town to the ice house. The ice house was a building about thirty feet long by ten feet wide with extremely thick brick walls for insulation. In the back were tons of ice blocks covered with burlap bags to help keep them frozen. When we told the owner how much ice we needed, he would just chop that amount off of the large blocks, carry it outside with a pair of iron ice tongs and hang it on the scales so he could get the exact weight. Then we loaded the block of ice in the trunk of our car for the trip home, again wrapped with burlap bags to keep it from melting. Once we were ready to begin the ice cream freezing process we put the ice in one of the burlap bags and, using the flat side of our large ax, pounded the ice into nice, even crushed pieces small enough to fit in our freezer. Adding some ice, some salt, more ice and more salt, then turning the crank of the freezer, again adding more ice and salt as it melted, we would get the entire process done in less than an hour. Then we would pack the can of ice cream in more ice and more salt to keep until we were ready to eat it. The wooden ladle had to be taken out first so we could eat what was left on it for a pre-taste of what was to come. We knew when we couldn't turn the crank any longer it had turned to solid ice cream. Little did we know or worry about getting sick from eating the raw eggs.

The only problem causing some concern to farm families was drinking non-pasteurized milk. That could be a problem for humans if the milk cows contracted a disease, then passed it on through their milk. We were especially aware of it since this did happen to a neighbor and good friend's family. Otherwise, everyone drank milk as it came from the cow. A mother and her son in this particular family were ill and bedridden for several months, however, so after that time they used only milk that had been boiled (pasteurized). We didn't pasteurize ours, but we kept a close watch on our herd of milk cows, testing them regularly for what they called "milk fever." I had to drink the boiled milk when I visited my friend, and since I wasn't much of a milk drinker anyway it was especially hard to get down. I didn't want them to feel bad because their milk was different, so I tried my best and usually managed to drink most of it.

There were some things, though, that I just couldn't force myself to eat—one was liver and one was what I called "scum" that formed on boiled hot chocolate. Another were lumps in gravy or puddings. I didn't like soft eggs either until I had that awakening from Bud's niece.

Food for our family and animals was priority so we were all involved, not only Mom and us girls, but the men played a big part in taking care of the garden as well. Uncle Joe didn't do much, but he liked to specialize like planting turnips in the fall. He prided himself in his technique of mixing the tiny seed with sand, then sowing both at the same time. He did raise extra good turnips which again, he loaded up in his car to take around the neighborhood. There were always more than enough since he planted turnips like he did everything—if a little is good, a lot is better. He liked to hear them brag about his excellent turnip crop which gave him the opportunity to tell them his planting technique.

Our garden produce started out the year with fresh rhubarb so during that time we had rhubarb every day—rhubarb pie, rhubarb cobbler, just plain cooked and sweetened rhubarb (which we ate with bread and butter), and rhubarb jam. Asparagus was ready about the same time as rhubarb so we had it every day as well, then we continued so on down the line. When strawberries were ready (and this was a duration of several weeks) we had strawberries plain, in cobblers, pie and lots of yummy shortcake until the end of the season produced smaller berries that we used for jam. Shortcakes were made from scratch out of rich biscuit dough, then spread with butter while they were hot and covered with sweet strawberries.

Our berry bed was so large that we had to pick strawberries every morning during the peak of the season. On those mornings everyone in our family got involved. We not only ate berries, but we sold berries and even let friends come in to pick berries. Strawberries are best, of course, when eaten right out of the patch—I should know. Since we each had our own area to pick, and it always seemed like my area had the smallest berries, I was known to sneak over into a different area to snap up the super big ones for my basket. The bigger the berries the faster my basket filled, but it didn't help; they just gave me another empty basket to fill.

When we rented our freezer in town we put up quarts of strawberries in glass fruit jars for freezing. Frozen strawberries to eat all winter was such an improvement over canned ones. Later in the summer we had cherries and peaches for the freezer as well. Vegetables were the same. When the peas were ready we had them every day, when the beans were ready we had beans, then in the fall it would be squash and turnips. Not that we had just those things to eat, but we had an awful lot of them when they were in season.

Lettuce and radishes were some of the first vegetables in the spring. We ate so much lettuce from the garden that I always thought it should be made into little bales so we could eat it easier. By the time each individual leaf of lettuce was washed and drained for our family of six, it took a lot of lettuce and a lot of time just picking and washing it.

As soon as our potatoes were large enough to start eating we would dig a few every day, many times cooking them along with fresh, young peas. Creamed peas and potatoes was a treat—my mother's favorite. Then as the summer went on and the potatoes grew larger we used them for every other kind of potato dish, but mostly mashed or fried. What potatoes remained in the garden at the end of summer we dug up and kept in the basement for winter use. We hauled bushels and bushels of potatoes in for storage, placing them in the coolest corner of the basement. It was also the furthest from the stairway. I always noticed that when I made one of my trips downstairs to get them for dinner. We used a tractor with a cultivator attached to excavate them from the ground for harvest, and then would pick them up by hand and toss them into bushel baskets and gunny sacks for hauling to the basement. My parents called our basement the "cellar," but for some reason neither my sisters nor I did. Apparently it was one of those words that changed from generation to generation. It took a lot of potatoes for all the meals we ate during the winter months, but still by spring there were usually enough left in the bin for seed potatoes to start the process all over again. Seed potatoes were made by cutting those leftover potatoes into small pieces making sure there was an eye (sprout) on each piece so it would grow. We had such a large patch that we used an old modified corn planter for planting. A couple of us would ride on the back of our old planter and drop potato pieces down through the openings. We kept turnips and squash in the basement as well, but since they didn't keep long we tried to eat them early in the winter.

Even though we had a very large garden, the weeding was all done with a hand hoe, plus, of course, the tried and true technique of hand pulling. When it came time for plowing and getting the ground ready to plant, we used horses or, in later years, our tractors. It was treated just like our grain fields—plowed, disked and harrowed smooth as soon as the ground was dry enough in the spring. Sometimes a little plowing was done in the fall, especially for areas we needed to plant early, like potatoes.

We planted the garden as soon as the soil was ready in the spring. Some things like potatoes could be planted early and still not be harmed by a late freeze, but warm season crops like tomatoes had to be planted later. Little caps made out of newspapers kept them from freezing in case a late freeze came along. These looked like little dunce caps and were actually made about the same way but they worked great for keeping the plants warm overnight. Then in the mornings we took them off to let in the warm sunshine. This gave the plants an extra early jump start on the season.

One tractor that was especially handy for garden work as well as other small jobs was our little bright orange Case—it was just my size, since I was about nine years old when they got it. I was so thrilled when I saw this small tractor out in our driveway that I ran out and actually just sat on the seat trying to visualize driving. Uncle Joe attached a wood platform on the back to make it easier for me to climb up to the seat. And, it wasn't long before I was driving it—I'm sure I begged and bugged my dad until he let me. Of course, it was convenient for him once I did learn because from then on I could help with the small chores before moving on up to the larger tractor to actually help with the heavy field work. None of our tractors had the convenience of cabs, radios or air conditioning—we had fresh air and sunshine without anything to disturb our time to think, sing or just enjoy the warm summer days. Every evening when we came in from work we parked the tractors next to our gas pumps, checked them over and filled them with gas so they would be ready for the next day. We had three gas pumps with underground storage on our farm so it was convenient. These all had to be pumped by hand, of course, by using the large iron handles pushing and pulling them back and forth until the clear glass upper storage unit was completely filled. When it was full, we could take the hose down and fill the tanks. Since there were no motors, I think they worked by gravity.

For a variety of meat we went fishing down in the river—usually a dozen times during the summer. Fresh catfish tasted mighty good. Catching them wasn't that much fun for me since I never seemed to be able to catch any. I sat all afternoon on the riverbank with a bamboo fishing pole in my hands just watching the bobber do nothing. Then that night in my dreams I would see my bobber, just bobbing along on the water ripples without any fish on my line.

When home freezers became available it took an extra large one to hold all of our produce, but what a great convenience to have it right by the kitchen on our back porch. The weekly trip to the locker was no longer necessary, and my trips up and down the basement stairs were much less. I missed the trip to town, but I sure didn't miss that cold time in the freezer or my trips down to the basement. It wasn't only cold in that freezer, but we had to keep the big, heavy door closed while we were in there. Everything was so white and frost covered it was like being in an igloo with our own key. It was one time we didn't have to be reminded to shut the door and turn off the lights.

At home we were constantly reminded of energy conservation—not that there was a shortage of electricity, but it was an expense farm families hadn't paid before. Power had been generated by windmills before that time. Farms were pretty self-sufficient. When rural electric came we kept lights off unless we were using them at the time—another one of Dad's rules. "Where you born in a barn?" my parents would ask if we kept the door open, letting in cold air during the winter months or flies during the summer months. It was another one of our parent's subtle reminders that sent us a strong and clear message.

Red Sun in the Morning, Sailor Take Warning; Red Sun At Night, Sailors' Delight

Those sweet children who were playing tag and running barefoot in the grass are back. I love to watch them play and laugh as they make up games and romp so carefree. I think they are looking for something in the grass—maybe they are looking for four leaf clovers. Maybe they are 4-H kids working on a project for the fair this year. I hope so. It is so much fun. I really should take something to the fair. What could I that may win me a blue ribbon? I think a jar of peaches or apricots would be nice, or maybe even an angel food cake. I could do that.

4-H programs were an important part of summer activities. Each month we not only had a meeting, but we did something fun along with it. Spring actively began with our April meeting that was held in the timber. We each took a large, clean can, some bacon, some eggs and whatever else we wanted to eat. By cutting a hole in the bottom of the can and setting it over a small fire, we could cook our breakfast on the top. After eating and our meetings were over, we spent the rest of the morning hiking in the woods picking wild flowers.

Once in a while, to make a little money for our club, we would put on a program to go along with our annual ice cream social. One year we held it in our yard with our front porch serving as the stage. It made a perfect stage with the big round columns used to hold the stage curtains. Our short plays might consist of five or six girls—if there was a man's or boy's part a girl dressed (and tried to sound) the part which made it all that much funnier. *Married to a Suffragette* was an example of the type of humorous plays we usually put on. This particular play was about "modern life" when the dad stayed home with the baby because his wife was a suffragette. I was actually still too young to belong to 4-H that year, but since my mother was the leader I was always part of it anyway. She was the leader for all of the years I remember from the time my older sister was old enough to belong until I was too old to belong. That covered many years. Other short plays would be something like *Yankee Doodle's Trip to Dixie* or *Aunt Jerusha and Uncle Josh*. In addition to the plays we had music, poetry recitals, or other dialogue followed with the ice cream, cake and pie. Nothing beats homemade ice cream, cake and pie. The 4-H fathers were fully involved in these programs as well by not only turning the ice cream freezers but helping with the seating which could be anything from bales of straw to sit on or bales of straw holding wooden planks to sit on. No matter, everyone had a good time.

    The 4-H program also sponsored a camp each summer. Even though I went several years, I only went one year as the camp bugler. Actually, it was a coronet that I played, but it was a good substitute for a bugle. I practiced playing the morning wake-up call and evening taps for weeks. My shyness surfaced again when it came time to assigning cabins so I somehow figured a way to stay in the same cabin as one of our club leaders that year who just happened to be Dale's mother. Even though I practiced for weeks before going to camp and could actually play it pretty well, I didn't think about how cold temperatures could be at six o'clock in the morning. The first morning I got out of bed, picked up my horn, went out to the little knoll where the American flag was raised and lowered each day, started to play and could hardly get out a weak squeak. Finally, I managed to make enough noise to wake everyone in the camp even though they had no idea what I was playing. That was a lesson for me.

By the time detassling ended, our skin was nearly as tan as it could possibly get. All of the girls put baby oil mixed with iodine on their skin to help the tanning process. I can imagine how hard that was on our skin, but it helped promote beautiful tans.

When possible, Elaine and I even went on dates together. When not possible, which was when she had a date and I did not, we liked to play tricks on her unsuspecting escorts. Many nights I would slip out to his car and hide in the back seat, hitch a ride to the movies and back, sneak back into the house when we got home, and he was never the wiser. What fun!

One year we convinced my mom and dad (we could be pretty persuasive at times) to take our family pickup to the state fair and stay overnight in the back end—four of us in that little pickup with straw for a bed. We couldn't even turn over unless all of us turned at the same time. It was a miserable and exceptionally long night, but fun. Dad was a real trooper anyway so he thought it was pretty funny. It was the last time we did it, however.

Our school had a good gymnasium, as large as any in our area so we hosted several of the annual basketball tournaments. During the girls' tournaments I was always playing, but during the boys' tournament games, I liked to just go watch. One year, Elaine and I decided to be janitors for the games so we could watch them for free. I know I could have gone to my dad for the money, but it was just one of those "experience" things, especially the two of us working together. We swept the floor at half times, before and after the games, we cleaned up the seating area and the rooms where the visiting teams stayed. There was only one shower area so most of the teams had to use classrooms for their locker rooms. It was fun, and lots of work—not real profitable, but fun.

My sister and Elaine's older brother were married while the two of us were still in high school. Elaine and I were both in the wedding as matching candle lighters. After the two of them graduated from college they taught school at a small high school about two hours away from home. When he came down with the mumps, they asked

PASSED THROUGH THE WINDOW ON MY WAY TO LIFE...

truck—a truck that had recently hauled pigs. It was mid-winter so we were just glad to get the lift even though it was a smelly one—especially for a town girl.

Once in a while, we delivered the morning papers for her brothers. This, again, was a new experience for me. Even riding a boys' bike was different. It took some getting used to, but since we were riding her brother's bicycle it was either ride it or walk. I opted to ride. Town life (even a very small town) was certainly different than I was used to on the farm.

Occasionally I helped her feed the gigantic dogs that her dad raised. They were superior bred St. Bernard's that had won several prestigious shows and boy, were they *big*. She wasn't afraid of them at all, but it put shivers up my spine just for them to look at me. Those dogs were so well cared for. Her dad actually planted a garden especially for their food so he could cook and can carrots and beans for them to eat throughout the year.

Detassling corn was an experience even for us—long days walking in the hot sun, early mornings and short lunch breaks. We had to get up at 5:00 in the morning, pack a lunch and walk downtown where we met our ride—a stock truck where we would all sit on the floor for our ride to the fields. Each group had a supervisor who checked our work and kept track of us. If we just happened to go over to another area to say, go to the bathroom and she couldn't find us, it was BIG TROUBLE. It was also trouble if we didn't get every single tassel and sucker. The suckers were short little plants of corn that had come up from the mother plant. Of course, these being close to the ground and the tassels being up so high we had to bend the corn stalks over to reach them, it kept us on our toes (literally) to not miss anything. By the time evening came and the truck came to take us back home, we were pretty ready for some rest. For some reason though, after a shower and a good meal, we sometimes had the energy to go roller skating the rest of the evening. It was a small rink in our small town, so it pretty much involved a lot of turns. In fact, it was all turns. We actually got pretty good by the time summer was over so by then we fell less often at least.

was behind a large two-story building that sat on the west side of the town square. Actually, the town wasn't large enough to have a square, but it did have a large building with one solid white wall. With white sheets attached to that outside wall, movies could be projected onto them. Wooden bench seats were set up between it and the building next to it for the crowd of people. How much better could it get?

Of all the days and nights Elaine and I spent together, and all the things we did together, it's pretty hard to sort out special events—each was special in its own way. She was part of our family; my dad loved to tease her. He called her "Elaine, Ilaine, Olaine" as he tried to scare her by putting white powder all over his freshly shaved face. She always pretended to be startled just to make him think he succeeded. He thought that was so funny he continued to do it every day, and every day she pretended to be scared.

Dad always shaved with a straight edge razor. The leather strap he used to sharpen it hung right by the sink where he washed his face after he was done shaving. Since his razor had to be sharpened each morning, it was almost like music to wake up to. One hand held the end of the strap tight while the other held the razor. Then in a rhythmic stroke, he would slap, slap, slap the razor against the strap until it was sharp enough to use. Every morning while we were upstairs dressing we could hear that scraping noise of the blade sliding back and forth against the thick leather, a subtle reminder of what other uses that old strap had as well. After a spanking or two with that thing we knew how bad leather could hurt bare bottoms; it only took a little threat after that. It was strong, thick leather, too. I never did see a new strap in all of the years he used it. That thing was indestructible.

Elaine and I played ball together in varsity athletics, we detassled corn together during the summer, we went to church together, swimming, sledding, skating—you name it. One day we ended up on the farm when we needed to be in town for practice, so we started walking the eight miles back to town. Well, actually, about three miles away from town a farmer gave us a ride in the back end of his

Don't Bite Off More Than You Can Chew

I soon found that the many school activities began to interfere with my down-home life of a farm girl once our country school closed and we became students in the consolidated town school. My inherent ability to have fun took over though with so many new friends that I thoroughly enjoyed it all through high school. Our recess times and physical education classes became more organized, with softball and basketball dominating.

It sure didn't take long for me to adjust to hot meals at lunchtime even though they were the butt of most students' jokes. I thought the meals were great, and was more than willing to eat any discards my friends didn't want. The school cook (the best) was the mother of my dearest, closest friend, Elaine. During high school, we were inseparable. Either she was out on the farm with me or I was in town with her. These were new experiences for both of us, but we soon adapted and had the best of both worlds, although I never did get used to her brother walking in his sleep. In fact, one brother walked and the other brother talked. I thought she had the great life living in town when she could go out after supper and play games with the other kids. When I was there we would play Kick the Can or Red Rover until it was so dark we couldn't see anything. It was pretty easy playing Red Rover in the dark if you were the one being chased.

The kids in town could even go to movies for a dime. The theater it was a pretty exciting event. We also marched at the front of the state fair parade each night walking throughout the grounds and ending up in front of the grandstand. We girls wore white blouses with full, gathered skirts made out of large farmer handkerchiefs—two had blue and two red. I had red, of course. Who ever heard of a blue bandana handkerchief in a real farmer's pocket?

4-H Rally Days were held in June when the clover was in full purple bloom. Since the four leaf clover was the 4-H symbol, one important highlight was the long thirty foot chain we made by tying together fresh swags of clover. During the ceremony, several members would weave the chain in and out as we went through our celebration of the clover routine. We spent the rest of the day playing games and swimming in the city pool.

I spent hours out in our yard looking for four leaf clovers. It helped that we had a high percentage of clover mixed in with our blue grass. Of course when I found one with four leaves, I picked it and pressed it in a book to keep for the good luck it was supposed to bring. That was before people began to use chemicals on the grass, as it killed out most of the clover and violets along with the weeds. Wild violets were normally purple, but we did find a few yellow ones once in a while. My sister and I experimented by propagating the two plants to grow a violet producing both purple and yellow flowers. We cut the plants down through the middle of the crown and tied them together some way. At least part of the time it worked.

In addition to hunting four leaf clovers, I spent hours laying in the grass just looking up at the clouds. It's a shame time has become so precious kids don't have time to just dream or look up at the clouds or find four leaf clovers. Even pulling weeds out of the bean fields was fun when we all worked together in the sun and fresh air.

PASSED THROUGH THE WINDOW ON MY WAY TO LIFE...

From then on I slept with my horn under the bed covers so it would be warm the next morning.

One other extremely popular 4-H activity was the annual basketball tournament for township clubs in our county. Some teams were actually very good since many farm kids played on the high school basketball teams. One time when our younger boys' club was playing, the leader asked me if I wanted to play. Of course I did. I was a member of the club so there were no rules against it—it had just never been done before. We absolutely trounced every team we played. I stayed down by the basket and shot the ball after my teammates got it and long-passed it down to me. Girls' teams only played half-court then so I wasn't very adept at dribbling the length of the court like the boys were, but I was taller so I could shoot over them. It was pretty funny. Our leader was so excited to win; he thought it was hilarious. We were so successful in fact that it wasn't permitted after that.

Playing basketball in high school actually was one thing I could do pretty well. Hard work and training had a lot to do with it, but I'm sure competing with older kids all the time, plus my many trips up and down the stairs at home helped as well. One year our team came within a few points of going on to the state championships. I was pretty short, but apparently the girls I had to guard didn't grow very tall either. My longer hair was a problem though, as it kept getting in my way during the games. Most of the girls had shorter, curled hair that stayed out of their eyes, but I had been through that "hair curling" procedure and wasn't about to try it again. One night my sister helped me pull it back away from my face, but she also pulled it up high on the back of my head and fastened it with a rubber band. Nobody had seen or heard of a ponytail so I was known as the girl with the "horsetail." It apparently was a first—at least in this rural area.

There were so many other 4-H activities we could take part in, and I tried to get involved in most of them. One was our county square dance team. TV was so new the year we danced at the state fair that none of us had it in our homes yet. When they televised us dancing us to come down and help take care of him while my sister was away teaching. Well, of course we jumped at that chance, it was a full week out of school! I was a senior, Elaine a junior, and as fate would have it the junior/senior prom was the day after we returned. As senior class president I was scheduled to be the master (mistress) of ceremonies. Since I had no time to prepare, the sponsor outlined it all on note cards so it worked out fine for me.

I was in band, orchestra and vocal music, however my contribution to band and orchestra would never have been missed. The reason I played the coronet was just because it was the same instrument a good friend played and we could sit together, only she was actually good. I was too timid to play it well and what's worse, for some reason our band instructor was always coming up with odd things for us to do—like whistling. Playing the horn was bad enough, but whistling? I couldn't get any noise out between my lips, and even if there was some way I could have, how do you whistle and giggle at the same time? I mostly just sat and watched that part. Even though I wasn't good playing the horn I did have a reasonably good voice, plus by that time I had taken a few vocal lessons. I was asked to sing on several occasions at school, but remember, it was a small school.

We had an excellent speech teacher in our small school who encouraged her students to participate in speech contests. Her students made fun of the way she talked with such precise, eloquent, correct grammar and thought it was intimidating. She also kept a box of tissues on her desk, constantly getting one out to wipe her nose. One year I did agree to participate in the division of interpretive reading. In this division, we were provided a book, given a short amount of time to decide what we would read and interpret before the judges. I'm not sure how much time we had, but when they came to my study room to get me I was taking a nap. I didn't get the highest ranking, but I did get second highest. I'm sure that was as good as I could have done anyway, even without the nap. The student helpers who came to get me thought it was pretty funny to find me napping before my presentation when most of the students were much too nervous.

Mom had always wanted to play the piano, but with her polio disability it was impossible. I guess that's why she was determined her own kids would learn how. It just wasn't something that I liked to do—an hour a day sitting at a piano to me was absolutely wasted time. Actually, none of us got very good, but we could play a little. At least my sisters enjoyed attending the piano recitals that I, on the other hand, disliked very much. We always had to wear our best Sunday dresses and act like little ladies for the whole afternoon or evening. That was tough, especially on a nice summer day when I could have been playing outside. Mother would convince me to take lessons for a while, then I would quit, then she would convince me to do it again, and that would work for a while, then we would start all over. Some of my piano lessons were from a lady who lived a couple of blocks from our dentist. That was convenient for my parents because they thought they could just drop me off for my piano lesson, then have me go on over to the dentist's house (he practiced in his home) for my dental appointment. They thought it was a good plan anyway, but should have known I could alter any good plan with a little ingenuity. The first time that plan was put into action, I just called the dentist, told him I was sick, and skipped the appointment. After that, I was hand delivered to the dentist. One time in particular, after having my teeth cleaned, I walked around the town square with the biggest smile you could ever imagine, showing everyone I met on the sidewalk my clean, shiny white teeth. Anyway, after a few years of on and off piano lessons, I reached the point where I could play for our little country church and Sunday school—that was enough to please her. After the elderly lady pianist passed away, I was the best they had available. It was the same with teaching Sunday school classes. Even when I was in school myself, I taught the pre-kindergarten class. They were the cutest, plus they didn't know more than I did, I don't think.

When I was in high school, aside from my feeble attempt at the piano and another fair attempt at playing the coronet, my music abilities were pretty limited. One year though, our county 4-H needed someone to sing the "4-H Clover Song" for our annual program and, wouldn't you know it, my mother volunteered me. At that time I hadn't taken any voice lessons, but that started me on the road to singing. Singing wasn't so bad—at least I could practice that on the run, so to speak, and not have to sit still. Plus, I had that musical training from my dad, singing while he planted corn.

Work Before Play

In addition to being the fly patrol and the chicken feather inspector, I was also the oyster watcher. Apparently, it was tradition that the youngest family members get the odd jobs. As oyster watcher, I made sure the oysters didn't overcook (or undercook) when we were having guests over for oyster stew. One pan held the milk and one pan the oysters, each with added butter, salt and pepper. When the oysters were curled up around the edges to perfection it was time the two pans of liquids could be merged together. We didn't want to add the hot oysters directly to cold milk or we would end up with curdled stew.

My dad's birthday was the last day in December so we had our annual oyster stew birthday party for him on that day. We also had oyster stew for our family dinner each Christmas Eve before we opened our gifts. That was an annual tradition as well.

One night my sister and I had to cook and serve waffles to Mom and Dad and their friends at their friends' home. There we were, in a strange kitchen cooking and serving waffles—just being little waitresses. There wasn't anything close to traditional about this setup. And, like when we cooked for threshers, we got pretty darned hungry watching them eat waffles, knowing we couldn't eat until they were done. We had a double emergency situation because the waffle batter supply was getting low. Since I was so afraid we would run out before I got to eat, I went in and told the four of them we were about out of waffles. I didn't see anything wrong with a little prewarning, but my mother was not happy with me at all. She told me, "That's not very nice," but I didn't know we could make more batter, and I was getting hungry for waffles. I thought it was about time they all shut down their eating and played cards.

One year we had grape wine with our Christmas dinner. Wine was something I hadn't often seen around our home. Since I was in my late teens at the time, I was allowed to have some with my meal. Actually, I liked dill pickles better, but I also had those—usually chopped up and put directly in my oyster stew along with chunks of celery, cheese or whatever was available. I didn't like the oysters anyway, so I ended up with a type of oyster stew vegetable soup.

One time we had some peach brandy down on a shelf in the basement. There was no mention of what it was there for, but I assumed some special occasion. There was also a can of pineapple juice on the shelf. One of my friends and I drank the pineapple juice one day and got into trouble. I can only imagine the trouble I would have been in had we drank the brandy.

My mother made several jars of grape juice each summer. Once in a while one or two of those jars would ferment a little. That was as close to grape wine in a non-alcoholic sort of way that I had tasted. She made grape juice by filling a half-gallon jar about a third of the way up with grapes, added boiling water to the top, then sealed the jar with a mason lid. After a few months, it was ready to drink. Any grapes we had left after making jelly was used for our juice so the amount depended upon the grape crop. We mostly got to drink the grape juice when we were ill. Our sick tray always included a large glass of grape juice along with a poached egg on toast, another sick bed staple. It was usually enough to make us well—at least feel much better.

Once in a great while, if some of his friends happened to be smoking, Dad would light up a cigarette as well even though he was pretty amateurish at it. To see him holding a cigarette between his thumb and forefinger with his other three fingers outstretched he looked more like he was holding a cup of hot tea. Then when he did take in a puff (I'm certain he didn't come close to inhaling anything) the smoke would just hit his mouth long enough for him to quickly blow it right back out again. He sort of looked like a steam engine going up a steep hill with short little puffs of smoke coming out his mouth.

    He thought it was funny to have me puff on his cigarette just to see me start spitting and choking. Apparently he had been around Bud too much, plus I think it was an educational lesson for me—he thought it would keep me from wanting to smoke when I got older, and apparently it worked.

Mind Before Matter

"Good morning, Ms. Rae. We are getting some pretty snow again this morning, and the forecast is for several more inches."

The nurse calls me Ms. Rae. She knows I like it even though she can only tell by my smile. I like snow, but I'm getting more anxious for the arrival of spring. It's been such a long winter here without anything to see through my window but snow. A few times I have seen kids walk by pulling their sleds. I suppose they are going over to the big hill in the distance for a day of sledding. That would be so much fun.

I had fun playing in the snow as a child, but I recall the warm summer months more vividly. Those activities remain so clear. Going to town on Saturday nights is one of my fondest memories.

After selling our eggs to the produce store we could do whatever we wanted before getting groceries, which was always our last stop before going home. If we had purchases to make such as shoes or socks, Mom made sure that shopping was done first before anything else. Buying shoes was fun even though I didn't like to wear them. At least in the summer I could get sandals, which weren't so bad. Buying anklet socks was an odd procedure: first we would double up our fist, then wrap the anklet around our knuckles. A perfect snug fit meant we had selected the correct size. After that we could walk around the town square or go to the movie (especially if it was bank night), or we may just sit at the drug store soda fountain drinking flavored cokes or sodas through a straw. Saturday night life on the town square was perfect leisurely summer fun.

Each summer we also had a family reunion in the city park—the same large family that went to Grandma's for Christmas and Thanksgiving. Reunions were lots of fun with more of that delicious food we always had for family dinners. The park had very few things to play on though—pretty much swings and a slide, and then there was the swing that had lots of iron things hanging down from the top. If I wanted to swing I had to grab onto the handle contraption while it was swinging around and around, usually with a lot of speed. This thing petrified me—it didn't help that I could hardly reach the lowest handle. Again, I was one of the smaller, younger ones so it was all I could do to keep my head out of the way of those heavy iron bars, with or without kids attached. Either way, I didn't care much for it. The slide was almost as intimidating. It was high, the sides were made of wood (the splintery kind), and the seat was hot metal. The problem with it was that once I got brave enough to climb the ladder, with all intentions of going to the top, there were so many kids lined up behind me I couldn't change my mind. So back down I went, only the hot metal way. That is, without holding on to the sides to prevent splinters in my hands. I soon learned that if I walked up from the bottom I could go as far as I wanted, then slide down from that point. It wasn't nearly as bad that way.

A Bird In the Hand Is Worth Two In the Bush

Actually, it was no surprise to anyone when I married a farmer and moved back to this home farm of many memories. When my dad asked my new husband and I to take over the farming so he could retire it was exciting, however, as things later began to change, I'm not sure it was the best decision we could have made.

We were married on the so-called "shoestring," but shoestrings went further in those days. It was great times and money didn't matter that much. The side by side work of farm families is something that money can't make up for—an experience I adored. It wasn't commonplace for women to work outside, especially in the fields, so I was sort of a pioneer by necessity even though I had driven tractors since I was nine years old. Back at that time it was mostly for pulling the hay racks while two men walked along each side tossing the hay bales up to one man on the wagon who stacked them.

Since stacking bales while riding on a moving hay rack with a hay fork in your hand was pretty risky anyway, I had to drive slow and steady, stopping and starting smoothly. It was perfect experience to learn tractor driving. After I was in my teens, I worked in a more important role, mostly disking and harrowing ahead of the planter. When I helped out as a farm wife, I added plowing and driving the corn picker to my "helper" duties. Actually, I was involved with about everything except the planting. With just my husband and I to do all of the work on our farm it was essential that I help out.

Our first big event came a year later when our daughter was born. It changed things a little, although she was born in the late summer months, giving me plenty of time to get back in the swing of things by the time the crops were ready to harvest. Childbirth was definitely something new to me. I had been present for the birth of baby pigs and baby calves but had no idea what those mothers had to go through in their own labor. I had a whole new appreciation for their pain. With suitcases packed for weeks and one false alarm trip to the hospital the actual time Mother Nature decided on finally came. How could something so tiny cause so much pain? But, of course, worth every bit. She came into the world with her big brown eyes wide open and didn't miss a thing from that day forward. With a couple of years behind us, we had enough money to feel comfortable purchasing toys. Her favorite was the spring-mounted riding horse that she rode with reckless abandon. Her sidekick was our German shepherd dog, "Tabby." Even though he was so much bigger, she soon had him sitting on command as she had heard us do. "Sit da down Tabby," she would say, and with a point of her tiny index finger she had complete control of this huge dog as he immediately sat at attention right in front of her small body.

With grandparents living close-,by she soon learned to run over to Grandpa's house to help him catch mice. It was amazing how much ground those little legs could cover when my back was turned. She didn't have to travel out on the road, so she wasn't in danger, but I always went to retrieve her anyway. It gave me an excuse to visit as well. This was her only set of grandparents to spoil her so they gave it their best shot. The mouse traps just had to be tended to every day, which I'm sure Grandpa used as an excuse for her to come visit. "Bampa catch mice" was her explanation for her daily visits.

Historically, farm life wasn't what you would call routine, however once rural people had access to better transportation, we enjoyed involvement in activities like everyone else. From the time our daughter was old enough to walk and talk she was in swimming, baton, music, Sunday school and later sports and 4-H activities. Like most farm wives, I spent a lot of time being a taxi service.

Thankfully, pre-school wasn't available, so I didn't have that drive every day even though it would have given her some playmates before she started to school. When she was old enough to attend grade school the bus picked her up at 7:00 in the morning and her school day wasn't over until 3:30.

It was a long day for a child. On her first day of kindergarten she surprised everyone by bringing a new friend home with her—not only a surprise to me but to her new friend's parents as well.

Like Looking for a Needle In a Haystack

Our hog operation was considered pretty big for those days since it was before confinement feeding and automatic feeders. This meant constant feeding, farrowing (birthing), sorting and, oh yes, constant fencing. We soon learned how hogs love to destroy fences.

In fact, five years after the birth of our daughter, and during the long days and nights of farrowing pigs, our son was born. We were out in the hog house until midnight, then during the rest of the night I had my own labor to enjoy. Our son was a complete opposite of our daughter. Light hair and blue eyes—and big. Also, he was the only baby in our local hospital so the nurses gave him their undivided attention. He was so spoiled by the time we got him home (in those days we stayed a full week), he thought being rocked was a way of life and expected it day and night. When he learned to walk (and run) over to Grandpa's house, his big sister was in school so he had to take over the "mouse trap watch" for her. We started the visitation trips all over again, only he wasn't as amused at the trapping part. Actually, he was more in favor of letting the mice free opposed to catching them.

He had two years to enjoy his visits before his grandpa died of a heart attack. That was a hard day, and unexpected, even though Dad had suffered one earlier attack just after we were married. With that first attack my mother called during the night and said Dad wasn't feeling well. After going right over we found him in pain and called his doctor. The doctor drove the fourteen miles out to the farm, examined him, called the ambulance and sent him right to the hospital where he stayed for several weeks. He recovered from that attack but apparently couldn't shake the problem completely. Sugar diabetes and a weak heart do not go well together, and he suffered from both. He was always pretty much of a homebody anyway, but after that he really balked at traveling. Mom's philosophy was more to go on the run all the time, but Dad's was more to stay home. In fact, he knew I would stick up for him so when he went to the doctor for checkups he would take me along. That way, when he didn't want to go someplace, off we would go to the doctor again, me as his witness.

Five years later on a sunny May morning, I saw a lady running toward our house screaming my name. I knew my parents had very good family friends staying over the weekend so I recognized her immediately. Since my husband and I were eating breakfast in our dining area she didn't have to run far. I knew immediately that something was very wrong and I was pretty sure it was my dad. I ran out the door and down the path to my parent's house. I don't think my legs have ever sprinted faster; it's like they never touched ground, but he was gone before I got there. Dad had made it as far as his car, but collapsed in the front seat. My mother had resigned herself to it, but, of course, I would not give up. I ran into the house and called the doctor to explain what was happening then went back out to my dad. I tried everything I could to revive him until the doctor got there and confirmed what we feared. By that time the weakness had hit my legs—I could hardly walk. My emotions were drained, my strength gone, so I just sat down with my head in my hands until I regained enough strength to go to the house. I didn't cry, but tried to stay strong and calm. Maybe it related back to playing basketball and my dad's strict training rules he had set out for me.

If God's Willing

(My mother always added "And the devil don't care," but Dad didn't especially like that part)

Things on the farm began to get more difficult after the death of my dad. A noticeable change began to take place as my mother began to age, and we no longer had Dad's strong hand of authority.

During this time of increasing difficulty, a personable young man came to our farm for a visit. Earlier in the month, he had read a newspaper article about our family that included a picture of me working in the field on our John Deere tractor. The article also included details about our kids' school activities and 4-H projects. He first showed me his identification as a photojournalist for the National Geographic magazine, or I may not have believed him. At the time, my husband and son happened to be showing one of our 4-H calves at the Illinois State Fair, so I visited with this young man for the afternoon. He was hoping to stay with us that summer, go to the livestock shows and write his story for the magazine. It would have been a unique experience to have him visit, especially having a story published in such a prominent magazine, but I felt our summer was going to be too busy with activities. Plus, our living style when we were showing cattle was much too primitive for most people. Our State Angus Auxiliary was hosting the bicentennial National Angus Show at the state fair. Being the current president, I was going to be extremely busy. As I look back, it would have been an interesting summer, and in a way I wish I had accepted his offer. Since the *Bridges of Madison County* book and movie came out a few years later, I can't help but wonder if that story may have been conceived during our visit that day. His questions about our covered bridge and its location (a mile from our farm), plus getting directions to drive there has kept me thinking often about this young man's visit.

As it turned out, we didn't stay in our tent that year at the fair, rather stayed in a close-by motel. Our convenience was much improved, and he would have been welcome. In the past, our sleeping quarters had been our small tent pitched in the cattle tie-out area. The tie-out area was a large piece of land on the east side of the grounds where the show cattle were stalled overnight. Rows of bright yellow straw beds lined the area during the day, then at night they were filled with cattle of all colors and sizes. Once in a while one would get loose and wander about the grounds. In a small tent like ours, we were always on the alert for any four-legged visitor walking through our tent in the middle of the night. Our only accommodations were our sleeping bags and clothing. Our only facilities were the bathrooms down on the grounds proper where we could also shower. There was no electricity available for lighting and no water for drinking. It was a pretty primitive way of camping to say the least, but it kept us close to our cattle in case any problems should arise. Tent camping was an improvement over staying in the back end of our truck as we had done previously. In those truck camping years, after unloading our cattle we simply tossed out the dirty straw, added clean straw, and considered it our bed.

Several years before we began showing cattle, and while our children were still quite young, we camped in the area that was actually reserved for camping. There we had a cement platform for our tent. We actually installed the platform one summer day by mixing up cement in a hand-cranked cement mixer. This thick base kept our tent up off of the wet ground, plus there was a bathroom and shower not far away—an important necessity when camping with young children. We even had cots to sleep on and ice chests for our food. With a gas camping stove we could heat water and cook food, so even without electricity we felt like we had most comforts of home. A few years earlier when our daughter was about two years old, we had her bed, her potty chair, her high chair, and even her little swimming pool all with us at our tent sight, but we were still over in an area without running water and electricity. She was so experienced in going up and down those long hills to the actual fair grounds that she learned how to run the brakes on her stroller. If she thought it was going too fast down the hill, she would just reach down and pull on the brakes. There was no worry on the long trip back up the hill—it went pretty slow when I had to push her stroller. That year, Uncle Joe came down to stay overnight. He was eighty years old that year, but he seemed to enjoy camping—he even enjoyed the long walks up and down the hills.

Anything Worth Doing Is Worth Doing Well

One year at our state fair the co-owner of our large black bull approached me at the last minute with the news, "You are going to show the bull today." Well, that was a shock to me, especially since I had never done it. I had never showed a bull anywhere, let alone the state fair, but I gave it my best try. It worked out OK, I guess; at least nobody said otherwise, plus the bull and I both came out of the ring together. That was all I was hoping for—I was definitely glad when the class was over. It's nothing unusual now for women to show bulls; it's done every day. That day was proof that anyone with the courage to try could do it.

Along the same line of not knowing what I was doing but doing it anyway, somebody suggested I show one of our German shepherd dogs in an upcoming dog show. He was a pretty good dog so I thought I'd give it a try. I thoroughly washed him (I figured that was an important step), brushed his hair as best I knew how, took him down to the show and actually did show him. Since I had no idea what I was doing, I just followed the same routine as everyone else. The poor dog didn't win—he wasn't last either, but he was spotlessly clean and well-groomed. I decided to take the same dog through obedience class. It was held once a week in what I later learned was a really bad part of town. Apparently I was safe with a big German shepherd dog guarding over me in the front seat of the car. The obedience training turned out to be more for me than for my dog; it led to me being the first dog obedience leader for 4-H kids in our county. The dog project has become extremely popular since that time, especially with kids who don't have facilities to hold large animals.

I tried being a 4-H leader for our local club, but with so many other activities I had to give it up. During that same time, I served on the county women's committee and the county 4-H committee, was an advisor to the university, and, of course, the revered "weather watcher." I'm amazed that I could keep up with all of it, but I was young and energetic. About my only real contribution to any of them happened to be during one of our county women's committee meetings. A Chamber of Commerce member presented future plans for celebrating the seven covered bridges in our county and asked for any ideas we might have. My suggestion was to set working exhibits up around the square much as they have in Branson, Missouri. This idea was adopted and the festival has been extremely successful since. I am disappointed that the commercial aspects of the festival seem to dominate more each year.

For a few years I entered the "Make It Yourself With Wool" sewing contest—a complete circle from my cotton bag sewing projects. Each contestant was required to make a 100% wool garment and model it before the judges. We were judged not only on construction but on the compatibility to our coloring, age and figures as we modeled. I never did win the contest (it was probably my modeling ability), but each year I placed high enough to receive more wool fabric to make something again the following year. We were also required to model our entry at the state fair in August, and with no air conditioning, wearing those heavy wool coats or suits made for an uncomfortable afternoon.

Since I enjoyed sewing so much, I was asked to be the moderator for the state plowing matches style show when it was held in our adjacent county. My daughter modeled one of her outfits for the show—she was six years old, so quite a hit with the audience.

Money Isn't Everything

"Ms. Rae, I think we should shut your curtains now. I know you like to watch out the window, but it looks like we are in for an old-fashioned thunder storm. I wouldn't want the lightning to hit you."

Oh my, the sky is getting dark. It has the look of hail and wind, which will not be good for our crops. We must have a good crop of corn this year to pay for our tractor. The bank won't like it if we don't pay them the money we owe them.

Fifteen years after we took over the home farm, a severe storm came through and ruined our crops. I was home alone with our two young children when the storm hit. I was accustomed to watching for storms, but this one was coming in from a different direction than I had never seen before. I knew it was a bad one since I couldn't watch it come up across the valley from the west. The sky got black and green as if it were night, only there were no stars or moon. I had never been in a tornado before, but I thought this storm had real potential. I only told my kids that we were going to the basement for a while, trying to stay really calm about what I feared. We sat down there on the basement steps for what seemed to be hours listening to first an eerie calm and then the strong wind blow, just wondering what was happening up above us. We had no electricity so it was pitch black, other than what we could see using our small flashlight. When I couldn't stand it any longer I left the flashlight with the kids and ran back up to look. It was still so dark out that the only time I could see anything was when a bolt of lightning provided a small window of light in the black sky. The wind was still strong, but the house was intact. I went back downstairs where the three of us stayed until the wind subsided enough to feel safe. When we did get back upstairs the sky was brighter, to the point where the sun was almost peeking through the remaining clouds. We could see that damage outside was pretty bad. Tree limbs were pounded into the ground, and pieces of tin were strewn about the yard. We later found that the tin had been grain bins which previously stood more than a mile away. At the time the storm hit we had ten very large elm trees in our yard, already weak from the Dutch Elm disease. Of course, they lost most of their huge limbs. Cleaning up after this storm continued on for three years just to get the yard back to it original beauty, but we were thankful to have the buildings saved.

That bad crop year was the beginning of our problems—the birth of a wedge that eventually came between my mother, my two sisters, and me. Even though the storm had caused our crops to be poor that year, it provided the opening, then each year it became more difficult to please everyone connected to our family farm. The drought of the next few years kept the farm income low while expenses continued to stay high. We continued to farm with the soil conservation methods and crop rotation as had been used on the land during the eighty years it had been farmed by my family. During this same time land grant colleges were, through their educators, teaching farmers to plow up more ground and farm it harder—the complete opposite of my dad's land stewardship. These new ideas sounded good to family members who had left the farm years ago, plus they were perilously influenced by the "farm expert" from the university.

As a result of these problems, we were very forcefully required to leave the home farm and find someplace else to live. There was nothing we could do—we were evicted from the home farm. Since we had no place to go, we asked about staying in the house and renting it by the month, but the new farm manager/extension specialist who was now employed by my sisters and mother, would not even consider allowing us that alternative. I believe his quote at the time was, "It's like a dog's tail, better to cut it off all at once rather than a little at a time." By this time we were middle-aged and past the time of starting over, so we had no idea what we could do. We were too young to retire and too old to start over. Farms to rent were scarce, if available at all, and we didn't have the money to purchase land. We did finally find a very small piece of land that included a house and barn. It was much too small for the machinery we had purchased to farm the larger home farm, also more expensive than we could really afford. But, it was a place to live until we could find something more suitable. We borrowed the money and purchased it. With only two months to find a place to live we didn't have many options.

I'm glad to have my window open again so I can watch the farming over in the distance. It looks like a good crop this year even though I just can't understand how corn can be planted in the same soil every year. Like people, I think soil should get some rest, yet the universities don't think so. God made only so much land—we must take good care of it.

The machinery I can see in the distance is so much larger than the tractor I loved to drive. Mine didn't have a cab or air conditioning or a radio. I enjoyed being out in the sunshine with the dirt settling over my tanned body. I doubt I would know how to drive one of these tractors. The sadness of leaving a family farm you have lived on for forty-five years, and that your dad, your granddad, and your great-granddad had farmed can only be realized by those forced to do it. It wasn't just me—it was also my husband and my kids who had lived there, so it was not easy for any of us. The new place was nice enough and the neighbors were great, but it was still so much different. We spent the rest of the year trying to adjust. I made the mistake one day of driving by the home farm we had left—it was already showing the hard use and lack of care. The farmhouse was getting run down and the once beautiful yard was filling up with junk. The good black soil that my dad and I had so often walked through barefoot checking for moisture was filling the roadside ditch from the fall plowing and wind erosion. I had to leave, and did not return again for a full decade. It was too painful.

Prior to all of this, life had been pretty simple. Farming had been rewarding. We had been married twenty-five years and lived on this—the only farm I had ever known. Along with being rewarding it can also be one of the more dangerous professions; we were so blessed to not have any major accidents. One of the closer calls happened one day when our daughter rode along with me to go pick up a load of fertilizer. While we were waiting in line, one of the large anhydrous ammonia tanks exploded, spewing the gas all over the area. We were blinded for a short while but managed to get out of the pickup and run—we didn't know where or even in what direction. I would open my eyes just a small squint to make sure we were on the street then continue running, pulling her along by her hand. Since the first direction we went was apparently with the wind, the strong fumes were simply following us, and we weren't fast enough to outrun them. So we changed directions, running about fifteen blocks before we felt safe. It was a few hours before our eyes returned to normal, but we still felt fortunate as some other customers were seriously injured.

I always worried when the kids worked around their calf projects, but thankfully they received only a few minor injuries. There were a few runaway calves, a few times they got knocked down and sometimes they got rope burns, but nothing worse. With all of the time spent working around cattle they never did get kicked hard, which is pretty amazing.

None of our accidents when working with calves can compare with some that my dad had years earlier when he was trying to break our calves to lead. One experience was the subject of my class essay when I was still in country school. It was titled:

Dad's Pets

As most all of you know leading a young calf is not so much fun. My dad quite agrees. Not so long ago dad put the leading halter on the calf and started off. They hadn't gone very far when they went by our bee hives.

Dad always kept three or four bee hives and was very fond of them. Most anything could happen, but the bees had to be cared for.

Now dad has never been bothered by bees. Neither had the calf 'til then, and then the calf took out across the yard dragging dad with him. Through two rows of shrubs and bushes, across the garden and back to the bees. Dad had to let go then. The calf ran for the bees and upset the box.

Dad, well he couldn't run quite yet, so he hobbled over and put the box up again. The next time the calf was led, did dad led it? Well, dad drove the tractor, and the tractor led the calf.

I'm not sure what grade this masterpiece received, but it did get a lot of laughter when read to the other students.

Don't Put All Your Eggs In One Basket

"Ms. Rae, I have your medicine. How are we feeling today? Maybe the sunshine will make you feel better. I'll just open your drapes farther so you can see out your window."

I am so glad she let me look out the window again so I can see the garden. The sunshine looks warm, as if spring were on the way. Spring is such a beautiful time of year with the rebirth of green grass and plants. It's time for farmers to plant their crops and time for the birth of baby animals. There is a large pasture over in the distance—maybe there will be some cattle out there grazing one of these days. I sure hope so. I miss watching baby calves play in the new green grass.

But our past enjoyment in farming was over. Our life had to go on; we were in our new home, both kids were in college now so we were going to try and make the best of our new life.

We had spent the first year trying to adjust to our new location and find our direction. The next year we were out West looking for calves when we saw a young bull calf that was nothing like we had ever seen before. He was unique in stature. We thought that with some good care and grooming he could possibly be a national champion bull. A couple of months later we looked at him again and he was better than ever; he was breathtaking. We worked an agreement with the rancher to bring the young calf to our farm in the fall as soon as he was weaned away from his mother. Our new acreage was so small that we were supplementing our income by purchasing young calves out West, then grooming them to sell for 4-H projects. This was hard work, but provided a living. So, of course, we were excited when this new bull calf came to our place to show and care for. He was fed the best feed we could buy; he was brushed and washed and walked and cared for every day. He was under a fan at all times and bedded with cedar wood mulch which circulated a sweet cedar aroma throughout the barn. We seldom left this new beautiful calf alone, and when we did it was for only a short time. He was getting bigger and better each day—people began to hear of him and were getting curious to see just how good he was. At the very first show we took him to as a calf he was the Grand Champion bull of the show.

The following winter when he was only twenty months old, we took him to the National Western Livestock Show in Denver. All of our time, work, expense and effort was there in one very, very large animal. Our nervous tension was pretty evident. Our nights were short since we didn't want to leave him alone any longer than necessary. The night before the show was especially short as our nervous excitement and worry kept us awake. It was so critical getting this calf ready for the most important show of his life. His hair was clipped to perfection; he was groomed in every minute detail. I usually handled the back end of the cattle by tying the tail switch up in a neat little ball, so I went about doing my part of the grooming procedure. When he was ready to go to the show ring he looked perfect, but he didn't like his tail tied up that day so he began swinging it back and forth like a bell. He was a big bull so we didn't argue with him about much—he pretty well got what he wanted. There were only a few minutes before the show and I wasn't sure exactly what to do, but I also knew I had to think of something pretty fast. So, I loosened the tie as much as I thought I could and begged him to stop. We were out of time and had to start walking him up to the show arena. We didn't know what he might do once he got in the ring, but we had to take that chance. The bull stood five feet tall now and weighed 2800 pounds, so if he wanted to swing his tail, he was going to swing his tail. Even so, we felt like our entire future was there for him to win or lose.

Our son was the only person we trusted to handle him in the show ring. In fact, he took time off from his college classes to fly out to Denver that day. As always, he was doing an excellent job even though handling a bull of this size was not easy. Partly due to the excellent handling, our bull looked so proud, as if he knew he was spectacular. He held his head erect and looked at the judge as if to tell him so. The judge gave him a good long look, stepped in behind him to watch him walk again, studying his every move. This was encouraging. So far, so good. As is routine, the bulls all lined up in a row one final time for review by the judge. Then he motioned our son to lead out into the number one placing as the winner of this class. The same routine followed for the championship, followed by the Grand Championship title. This beautiful young calf appeared to be enjoying the challenge. The large crowd of people became silent as the judge went to the microphone for a few last comments. My knees were weak and my hands were sweaty, even in January. One final comment, one final look, then he walked up to our son to shake his hand in "congratulations." He had won the Grand Championship honors at the National Western Livestock Show. This was an immense victory and we were so grateful. It was difficult to hide our emotions—our daughter was standing by me during the festivities so while publicity pictures were being taken of the winners, we both cheered and clapped our hands until they burned. When we returned to the cattle barn everyone celebrated our victory—the entire group of exhibitors enjoyed food, drink and, of course, discussion about the show. We thought our worries were over and our future was once again bright.

However, this was another one of those lessons in life. Since our bull was now a National Champion, we just assumed purchase orders for his semen would come flooding in. Well, we learned that just being a winner wasn't enough. We had a lot more work to do, only this time involving promotion and selling. We were too well aware that we needed these sales to help pay expenses we had incurred in caring for the bull, plus paying for the small farm we had just purchased. We were also aware that the bank would be pressing us to pay off our loan, so we had to think of something to do. With jugs of frozen semen in the back of our pickup, my husband went out on the road to sell. He went all throughout the West, covering much of the ranching country in the United States. The ranchers were receptive and anxious to use this new champion bull—next year we would know enough to start our semen sales earlier in the year. All-in-all, things went pretty well.

While my husband was out selling, I talked with our banker to apprise him of our recent good fortune and what we were currently doing. He agreed to extend our loan since the bull was bringing in money and doing so great. He even agreed to lend us any amount of additional money we needed to promote the bull. The down side I learned during our meeting was that he required me to sign an additional mortgage on my home farm—the one we had just left. That part was a big concern to me, and I had to think about it. But what choice did I have? The farm was my home, and it didn't seem right to put any risk on it, but we had to live, so I signed the note. I later realized that my hesitation that day had merit. Even though this loan officer seemed too nice to do anything leading to my detriment, it was a bad decision on my part.

But, not long after that day, the bank started requesting us to pay off the entire balance of our livestock loan. They had to be aware that there was no way we could come up with the money. Why was he calling in the loan now, just when we had the business potential set to pay it off? The value of machinery was going down and average livestock valuations were dropping, so selling off our inventory wouldn't even bring in enough money. We didn't want to sell our champion bull since he was our future source of livelihood. But, we were forced to do something and finally decided we would have to sell an interest in him or lose him entirely. The banker did agree to wait for the money until we could make the sale and get something worked out.

Since we had earlier talked with a successful rancher, who was interested in purchasing part of the bull, we contacted him again to see if he was still interested. He was, so the sale of an interest was worked out and finalized. It even seemed to be fine with the bank; that would be great and everything would be clear as soon as we paid off the loan. We were getting the paper work all done with the rancher—everything seemed to be working out finally, and the future appeared brighter than it had for a long, long time.

A Penny for Your Thoughts

"Ms. Rae, look at your beautiful bouquet of flowers that just arrived. Red roses that you like so much, and it looks like somebody knows how well you like farm animals. See, the vase is a baby pig. Isn't that cute? You had lots of baby pigs when you lived on the farm, didn't you?"

I like baby pigs. Once I had a piggy bank that was stuffed full of pennies. He won't ever be hungry again, but I wonder where he is—maybe he's in the closet where my blue dress is hanging.

It was especially quiet that hot summer evening since it was too early for the frogs in the nearby pond to sing their raspy music. I was in the kitchen cleaning up after supper, actually enjoying the quiet solitude. Suddenly, somebody was pounding on the front door. My heart leapt up into my throat and caught there for a few seconds. Nobody ever used the front door. I was really glad that my husband was home. As he opened the door, the small glimpse of light was enough for me to see the sheriff's car parked in our drive. Why was he pounding on our door? Was somebody hurt? What was wrong? All of these thoughts raced through my mind. I hurried into the other room to see, yet afraid to find out. When I got in there he was reading something. When he saw me, he handed me a paper and continued to read the notice that the bank was going to sell my home farm at a public auction—the one I had just signed a mortgage note on. They were also going to take our livestock. That was quite a birthday present for my husband as it was his birthday that day.

The years of work and recent frustration rushed through my head like a giant, three-dimensional cartoon flick. The happy, the sad. It all became blurred as the tears started sweeping across my eyes. Knowing that it was going to be hard on my husband, I tried not to let him see my emotions.

The farm had been in my family for the entire century, and I knew of the pride and independence bred into farmers. Their constant battle with Mother Nature seemed to give them each a sense of independent obligation to control adversity, so it was going to be hard to let it go.

The sheriff finished reading, said goodnight, and drove off. Neither of us spoke much the rest of the evening. The void was evident, but what can be said at a time like this? The reality of the present—the insecurity of the future. It was like a blanket of heavy fog.

After my husband had time to silently sort through everything in his mind, he finally broke the silence, "What are we going to do?"

"We are going to fight this. We can't let them do any more to us. We have to fight it," I answered back, hoping it would instill a little hope.

As I had feared, emotionally beat and exhausted he murmured, "We can't. We don't have the money to fight it. They have stopped us from doing anything." Even if I did feel the insecurity, I didn't dare let it show. I had to appear stronger than I actually was.

We couldn't understand why the bank was doing this now—just when we had the chance to pay off the balance of our loan. They knew we were taking in money, they knew we had a good share of it in our account at the time—just not all of it. Why had our banker changed his mind so suddenly? Checks for semen sales were coming in, but the foreclosure action only gave us twenty days and we were still $15,000 short. We were so worried, but tried to hide our anxiety. Our kids had enough to think about with schooling, looking for work, and everything else young people worry about. Even so, we couldn't keep it from them any longer as things began to get worse.

Neither of them had ever asked for much. Our daughter was always happy with her homemade clothing, and our son had never asked us for much either. It should have been no surprise that they were so much help to us in the days to come. One day would be a big high and then the next day a deep low. Money would come in the mail, but then so would the bills. We were taking more and more antacid pills. There were times I feared of what my husband may do. There had been more than one farmer end his life during these bad times. I had to try and keep him upbeat and in a positive mood. We were down to five days and still short $3,000.

The next day the phone rang—it was the bank teller.

"We have a check over here that you deposited, but it won't clear. We are sending it back and holding that amount out of your account," she said.

"Oh, don't do that," I told her, "I'll be right over to pick it up." I knew it would take too many days to float that check around in the mail and during which, time would run out for us. It was not customary procedure for this bank to send checks back when they didn't clear the first time. Usually they would run them through at least twice. Why were they doing it this time? I began to get very suspicious and wondered what they were trying to do. We drove right over to the bank so I could pick up the check. It was getting near closing time so we didn't even take time to park the car—I just got out at the street and ran up the walk. When I found the teller who had called me, I picked up the check, but I also asked her what the balance was in our sales account. This was the special account we had set up for collection of semen sales money. She checked the computer, wrote some numbers down on a piece of paper and handed it to me. $5.85 balance.

"This can't be right," I told her "It's short $10,000, even without the check you said you were sending back." I was devastated. By that time my husband had parked the car and walked into the bank. When I told him what had happened, he leaned on the desk, pale and weak. It was too much for him to handle. Things weren't adding up—what was going on? The teller asked me if I wanted to talk with the bank president; of course I said, "I sure do." She went to the phone to call him, came back to me and said that he had taken the money out of our sales account eight days ago. I took the phone to ask him directly why. He told me he didn't know it had been done until just now but by that time I was having a hard time believing much of anything. I pleaded with him to put the money back in our account so we could use it to pay off our loan, however, he assured me that they were not required to do so. This was really getting me upset. It seemed they were deliberately trying to keep us from paying off the loan. Why? I asked him again to put it back in our account, and one more time he declined.

It was a long trip back home for only being a few miles. During the entire trip I kept wondering if there wasn't something we could do. I guess by nature I'm somewhat of a fighter, and fight hard before I give in. Being the youngest in the family I had to be. I'm not usually hesitant to ask for help from the most official person I can find either, so I started looking in the phone book until I found the banking department for the state. That appeared to be a pretty high authority, so I called them and explained to them what had happened. They told me that the bank was way out of line. Apparently it was a higher authority than I even realized because the money was put back into our account the next day.

That was a breather, but we figured we didn't dare risk leaving the money in that same bank account again. We decided to pay off as much of the loan as we could even though we still didn't have the full amount. We couldn't chance them taking the money out again and doing who knows what with it. Even though they had assured us that it wouldn't happen, we did not trust them at this point. We went ahead and paid off as much as we could with only four days left. There was still the matter of the check that I had picked up from the bank teller. It wouldn't be enough, but it sure would help. By then we didn't know who we could trust, and since the bank the check was written on wasn't far away, we drove down to see what had caused the problem. As we suspected, the money was there and available. This time we had them give us a cashier's check, which was fine with them; we were more than ever doubting the integrity of our local bank. We were convinced that for some reason they did not want us to pay off our loan. We had three days left and still needed to come up with a little more money.

We didn't want to ask anyone, but were desperate, so we did call one rancher to see if he would pay us for the semen he had purchased in the spring. He agreed to send us the money right away. What a relief. This would do it. This would be enough to pay off our loan and save our cattle, our bull and, of course, our land.

The next two days seemed like two decades. The money just had to get here before Saturday morning or it would be too late and the bank would have what they apparently wanted. The twenty days would be over. Our son was waiting at the mailbox when it came on Friday. "It's here," he yelled as he came back through the yard. This was one of those good mail days. He ran into the house carrying the small white envelope, waving it in the air. I could feel my heart pumping as I opened it, half way expecting another disappointment. But, it was there. What a relief. The money we needed was in my hand. Before reality set in we all collapsed for a few minutes. Of course it wasn't over yet—there was still the final payment and the paperwork that had to be done. We didn't even enjoy another minute of relaxation. We got in the car and went right over to the bank before the bubble could burst. Our son stayed to do the work at home while we went over and met with the bank president again, for what we hoped would be the last time. I had the exact numbers figured on paper, but ,of course, he re-figured them. We paid the amount we had both agreed upon and then asked for the papers canceling our security agreement that would clear everything for us. We wanted to take it right over to the county court house to get it filed. The bank president said he didn't have the papers there at the time, but would mail them to us the next day. Also, he said that there was no need for us to take them up to the courthouse to be filed. We were so happy and relieved that we didn't argue the matter, however, we did go on over to the courthouse to record our payment anyway. We had learned a few things during these past few months, and one was not to trust anything to chance. What a relief. A load had been lifted. Our livestock was free so we could set about paying off the other loan and getting my land freed from the bank as well.

A week went by, yet the papers had not arrived. Had the bank president forgotten? After days passed I called to remind him we had not received the release papers.

"The loan committee decided not to release your security interest in your livestock. You will have to pay off your real estate mortgage before we can do that," was his response. Of course, by having access to all of our financial records, he obviously knew we did not have the money or we would have already paid it. I was so dumbfounded; I reminded him he had promised. My voice was shaky and so were my hands as I tried to take notes while he talked on the phone. As I scribbled them on paper the family was reading over my shoulder to see what was happening. I'm sure my trembling made them aware that it was *not* good. At that moment it seemed like it would be too much to fight this any longer and just let them have it all. It seemed to be what they wanted. I don't even recall the next few days. That time was a blur, but it didn't seem right. Just in case they had changed their mind, I called up to the county clerk to see if anything had been cancelled. It didn't surprise me when she said, "No, it hasn't," but it did surprise me when she added, "I think you need to contact a lawyer." Apparently, even she knew that things were not done as they should have been.

This was the beginning of the most education I have received during my entire life—good and bad.

Most of my connection to lawyers had been through my dad and uncle while I was a young child. Sometimes when they went up to see their attorney they would take me along. I didn't know much of what they did up there, and really wasn't interested. It was a trip to town.

An Ounce of Prevention Is Worth a Pound of Cure

I'm not sure where it came from, but apparently my sense of trust was slow to sour. I had always trusted people. Even when my uncle passed away and his estate was in question, I was willing to concede it to be only a mistake. That foul taste came back hard and fast though when we began having our trouble with the bank.

That past experience effected my determination this time to carry out any legal means necessary to prove us right. Apparently I got my grandmother's determination as well as her physical attributes. There is a time in life when one has to stand up to the establishment and push aside that huge foot that seems to have you squashed into the ground. We began the search for an attorney.

Contacting a lawyer? We had no idea how to go about finding legal help, but that was the beginning of a learning experience unequal to years of schooling.

Since there was a university in a nearby town that graduated excellent attorneys, I called them for suggestions. They made some recommendations for attorneys but as we went down the list one had a conflict and the second one should have had but didn't tell us. The next one was one of the professors who was supposed to have lots of experience with banks. That sounded good to us so I got an appointment with him. By this time my nerves were so bad that I couldn't force myself to leave the house. It made me feel terrible that I wasn't able to go, but the highs and lows of the past few weeks had been too much. My husband and son went without hesitation. I'm sure they had to be aware of my nervous condition even though I tried to hide it. All summer had been a time of worry. Would we lose everything? Would I lose the farm where I had lived my life, my father had lived his life, his father and my children?

During the hours they were gone my mind was jumping around like a rabbit; I couldn't help but think back to the years of farming, wondering if we could continue, and if we couldn't, what we would do. Our entire family would be lost since this was our life. We loved the cattle business, plus it had been such a long struggle to get to the height of success. For years we worked with our cattle trying to breed them for improvement—trying to get to the point of raising superior breeding stock. We struggled with breeds of cattle, the best breeding lines, and studying the good and bad traits of all breeds. Our entire family worked at it and contributed long hours, late nights, and early mornings working with calf projects to make them the best possible. Both of the children had been willing to add the extra time necessary for quality, championship cattle and that was in addition to all of their school activities. It was exciting for all of us when they could claim a championship and we could forget for a short time about all of the hard work. In the last few years we had finally reached the top—the best in the nation. The first came with the National Champion female and the following year our National Champion bull.

It's a great feeling to see your cattle led out before the judge and have him congratulate you for having the best. A champion bull with the superior genetics is just what we needed to collect enough money to pay off the bank. With this we were just beginning to reap the rewards of time and work. Semen sales were starting to take off; now why was the bank trying to stop us?

It would have been great had the first attorney we contacted been able to handle the case, but his conflict prevented it. My husband and son had gone into town to meet with him and were so impressed with his knowledge, yet disappointed when he couldn't take the case. He wasn't asking for a large retainer up front either, but he couldn't represent us, so we had to go on from there.

Just as I was deep in the thoughts of the past, my husband and son returned from the lawyer's office and the present problems returned to my mind. The guys seemed happy as they walked to the house. Yes, they were happy. The lawyer had told them that the bank would have to release everything—they were clearly in the wrong. The lawyer was even willing to come out to our home to visit with me since my phobia had returned and I wasn't able to use elevators. His office was on the tenth floor so it was impossible for me to walk up the stairs.

Phobias apparently come back into your life when something puts you in a lot of stress. The phobia that had come back to haunt me related back to my childhood days when, as the youngest, my sisters loved to tease me in a variety of ways including holding me down under blankets to hear me scream. Scream I did, because it terrified me. They also instilled a fear of water by holding me under the water faucet to hear me scream. I must have done a lot of screaming when I was a child. No wonder I spent most of my time outside the house where it was safe.

Eventually there is opportunity for revenge on older sisters as they were dating while I was still young enough to be a pest. My favorite revenge was accomplished by putting two case knives (the kind not sharp enough to hurt anyone) up over the kitchen door as I shut it. This made a nice little shelf for anything I wanted to put up there—usually I tried to find the best noise-making utensils in the kitchen like more silverware, pans and small measuring cups placed on a large tray or cookie sheet. If I was really mad at them, I might just add a little water in one of the pans. Then, when my ever-teasing sister arrived home from her date (the later the better) and opened the kitchen door, it sounded like the entire house had fallen down. Everyone, including my parents, would wake up, check the clock to see what time she got home, and I would have a good laugh before going back to sleep. Oh, what joy! It was at least a step toward my sweet revenge for their constant teasing. Any further revenge I dreamed up couldn't make up for what they had forced on me—I guess they just liked hearing my screams of terror.

One of their favorites (and my most disliked) was holding me down in a rocking chair and singing, "Rock-a-Bye baby, on the tree top. When the wind blows, the cradle will rock. When the bow breaks, the cradle will fall, and down will come baby (usually they substituted my name), cradle and all." This irritated me to the point I would scream, fight to free myself, and then run as fast as I could.

The irony of it was that one of my favorite places to play when I got a little bigger and tall enough to reach the lower branches was high up in the tree top. A large maple tree (one moved there with the house) was just outside the kitchen door and was perfect for climbing. One lower limb on the tree was just the right height for me to jump up and reach, probably about six feet from the ground. I could then pull myself on up, but it wasn't so low that I would drag my head on the ground when I hung upside down by my knees. The other branches, all the way to the top, were placed just far enough apart for me to reach with ease. From the top vantage point I could see the entire river bottom for about twenty miles. What a view. Time went by way too fast until I got called back down to come in and eat or do some kind of chores. When I sat in the very top where the branches weren't as strong, I could move them back and forth in a swaying motion. It was almost as if I were rocking in the chair that made me so angry a few years earlier. It was my own little world up there, and I was in complete control of it. Nobody else had the courage to climb the tree and get me. My mother always told me I would fall and break my neck but I never did, thankfully.

You're Never Too Old to Learn

Part of my trust was instilled in me because everyone in our farming community was so trusting. Even though we were out in the country, at that time there was a house about every quarter mile. We felt safe and assured that if we did have trouble, help was close by. Between houses there usually was a friendly farmer out working in the field, so we had no reason to feel insecure.

I did come home from school one day to find a man waiting for my parents. In my trusting, normally friendly way, I sat on the tractor and visited with him until they got home. He was a sad case, having suffered too much mental pressure during the war so was forced to live his days in a mental security institution. He was an old friend from my parents' youth, so our farm was usually his first stop on his short trip of freedom. Every once in a while when opportunity presented itself he would walk, ducking in and out of standing corn and heavy timber, the sixty miles back to the neighborhood he remembered. I wasn't aware of this until that day when my parents came home to find me visiting with this fellow. Our visit didn't make much sense to me, but then he probably wasn't getting much out of my conversation either. He told me about the guns he had and the problem he had with the local authorities and how he was going to "get them." When my parents found me visiting with him I guess they decided they better tell me the entire story, so from then on I was a little more careful when strangers came to visit.

Apparently, the local authorities were the bad culprits who took him to the institution, so he was not about to forget their part in his plight. The problem was that he always wanted my family's help to get his revenge. We never could figure out how he managed to get weapons, but we didn't question it either. It kept us all pretty alert (including me) after that.

A Penny Saved Is a Penny Earned

Well, my guys seemed to be satisfied that this attorney was capable of handling everything so we continued to take care of our livestock sales. We sold as many cattle as we could by taking them to special sales. These sales brought in a few more dollars. After our son graduated from college we depended on him to take care of things at home so I could go along and help. One thing about growing up as a tomboy, I was not only used to the long hours, but had developed strong muscles as well. I was comfortable working with dirty straw, cleaning up after the cattle, washing and drying them, and was also used to the smell of the barns where they were stalled. Actually, I enjoyed it all, including the smell. Grooming cattle is a hard business to learn and is exceptionally specialized. It takes a special ability to know what to do and when to get the best appearance for your animals.

A very good friend had helped us through our first years of learning the business. He not only knew the tricks of the trade and was willing to help us learn, but has been a big inspiration to our entire family. As a child, polio crippled his legs and one arm, making everything he did more difficult, still he never complained. He was one of those unique people you meet once in a lifetime. But, there were those days when I wished we hadn't learned the business since between all of the great times were some bad experiences. One time our son's calf knocked him down in the show ring, and once there was the calf that would not mind our daughter so "Dad" had to show her how it was done. Of course, the calf ran away with him, too; that was one of those times when you wanted to laugh but didn't because you knew better.

Since I was physically strong it was handy for me to help my husband load and unload all of the equipment. "Oh, I felt something pop in my back," I said, and dropped the large box I was helping load. That did it. I don't know how, but he loaded it himself with me watching the rest of the day. He knew what a sore back was like since he had been hit with a baseball in high school and suffered pain for several years because of it. I figured a few days of rest and I would be back to my normal strength, but it didn't happen that way. My injured back was not improving, however, since it wasn't completely "kaput" I continued to do as much as I could.

After five months of aggravating it, I couldn't walk. We didn't have the money for treatments, and we had no health insurance. One day our daughter called and said she had an appointment for me with her chiropractor.

"Oh, I don't think he can help me," I told her, but being the insistent person that she was, she refused to listen to me. I did go as she ordered, and had the x-rays of my back. They showed several problem areas requiring $1,200 in treatments to get me to the point of walking again. We didn't have that kind of money, but we agreed to the treatments. I had learned over the years to not question my husband when he sets his mind on something. Sometimes he could be persuaded, but I could see this was not one of those times.

My bad back only added to our already existing problems; not only were my nerves bad, but my husband's were becoming worse each day. I couldn't convince him to get help. Some days he would just explode over small things to vent his emotions. At times he would leave for hours at a time and just walk. Times were tense between us, and our entire family was feeling the pressure more each day.

Once in a while we could laugh at everyday events, forgetting our problems for a while.

"What in the hell is wrong with me? I burn and itch all over!" My husband was wiggling and scratching his body as he came stumbling out of the bedroom. I really had no idea, but it was such a funny sight that I couldn't speak anyway. Everyone burst with laughter but nobody could come up with any reason. The closest guess was from a friend who happened to be staying with us at the time. He suggested it was the laundry soap I'd used, which seemed so logical we left it at that. Later in the evening I went into the bathroom and it hit me. "Did you take a bath in the tub?" I said as I again started to giggle. I had used bathroom cleanser (the stout kind) to clean the tub earlier and had forgotten to rinse it out. He had taken a bath in cleanser! Well, he ran to the basement for a shower as fast as he could get there to rinse off the cleanser. At least it was a break from our other worries that normally consumed our days.

Since we were trying to save money every way possible, we kept some clothing past its normal usefulness, but my mending skills weren't as good as my sewing. One time, when trying to mend my husband's pants pockets, I sewed them shut—the two front pockets. Every time he tried to put his hands in his pockets, they would slide right on past. He would normally growl, and the rest of us would laugh. It was one short funny moment each time he did it.

We were also starting to give up on the college professor/lawyer we had already paid to help us. He seemed to be at an end of what he could do, and we feared that he was getting us into more trouble than we already had.

"We can't continue with him" my husband said after one of our appointments. Fighting a bank in court just isn't an easy thing to do, so we definitely needed good representation who would not buckle under. It seemed all laws in the world were written especially for the benefit of banks. If we hadn't been so desperate we may have given it up, but as it was, we had to keep trying. It seems when we first talked with attorneys they were full of ability, but then showed the same weaknesses after speaking with a bank executive or, of course, their legal counsel.

The next attorney was okay for a while, but after a few months we saw no results again. Everything that had happened was bad. He simply didn't have the ability to handle it. We thought that after so much time had passed and he still hadn't met with us long enough to get the details, we just as well not depend on him any longer. He hadn't charged us much since apparently he knew his value was worthless. It's as if the bank knew our dilemma and decided this was a perfect time for further actions. There seemed to be no way we could stop them now.

But once again we set out to find legal representation. It was common in those days for farmers to require services of attorneys to help with their farm problems, so in another attempt to find counsel, we sought recommendation from a friend. Of course, we contacted this attorney right away and made an appointment to see him. We gathered up all of the papers we could find trying to get them into some type of organization before we went down to our appointment. He listened to our story, looked at the stack of our organized papers and sternly said "Folks, you don't owe that bank one damn cent. You have been damaged by their actions and we are going to fight this thing." What music to our ears. He had listened to our entire story of the past few years and actually saw the picture as we did. We were so happy and relieved. We knew there was a long battle ahead, but at least there was going to be a battle. Now we had to find a way to accumulate money to pay the retainer fee of $10,000 he requested. That was a lot of money, especially at this particular time after what we had just gone through paying off our bank loan.

This time we were pretty sure the attorney had our interest at heart. Time would tell—and it did—some good and some bad. But at least it was a start in the right direction. His first comment to us that we didn't owe the bank any money was good enough for us, but is was obvious he was going to be expensive. That was a major stumbling block for us, of course, but figuring that you get what you pay for, we were determined to give it a try.

Before he would even begin to work on our case, we had to get him his retainer fee. Our only hope by this time was to file a lawsuit back against the bank for damages which he planned to do just as soon as we paid him. This time we hoped it would be the answer to our problems since we were running out of time, and definitely out of money.

Less Talk, More Work

These were the "days that try men's souls" so to speak—days of absolute disbelief! Just about the time we thought everything was under control, something else would happen to bring us suddenly back to the reality of our situation. The farm and ranch economy was the worst since the depression of the thirties. My parents had told me horror tales of those days time and again and even though I pretended not to listen, I recall them vividly. Many people have related to those times, but in some aspects this depression was harder on farmers. There are so many necessities in the current era like insurance, taxes, and every day living expenses. Many of our friends were so depressed—many sold out, losing farms that had been in their families for generations. Some that were unable to handle the depression took their own lives, and some took the lives of other family members along with them. It was a sad situation for many.

"The bank knows we can't hold out for long," my husband said one day, so I could see he was beginning to question again the risk of going through with it. Should we just give up now?

"I'm too old to do anything else but farm. Nobody wants to hire an old man," he said. I didn't say so at the time, but I had been thinking seriously about trying to get work just as soon as I could get my back strong enough and, with the medication I was taking for my nerves, I thought I could at least try. I had the same problem as he did with age being a factor, but I could always work as a waitress if my

PASSED THROUGH THE WINDOW ON MY WAY TO LIFE...

back would just get strong enough to handle the heavy work.

So, we went out on the road again to get money for our legal expenses. Traveling was expensive, but any little profit would help. It not only helped financially, but it was a help to our mental attitude. There were at least partial days when stress could be put aside and we could regain our pride and sense of accomplishment. Selling was difficult, but at least we felt like we were doing all we could. We felt blessed that we had this to do—most farmers did not.

One of the not so great possessions we were forced to keep whether we wanted to or not was the old red pickup truck. Not that it was all that old, but it just as well have been. Every six months it needed more repairs. It should hold the record for the most new motors and clutches in one vehicle during a five-year lifetime. Just as with our cattle, the bank would not release our pickup, so we could not sell it, trade it, or give it away. We just kept putting on new parts. We always carried a heavy rock in the back end to make it ride easier. Traveling the countryside, many times out in the large sand hill country, in a ton truck isn't exactly a comfortable ride. It kept me fully aware of the pain I had in my back.

I'm so sure that truck just waited to break down at the most inconvenient places. Instead of breaking down at home, it always waited until we were far away in some small town in some other state. It became a challenge to spend days waiting for repairs and not get cabin fever—I wasn't good at adjusting to things like that, especially when I didn't know what was happening back home. It was for sure we had enough money in that old pickup to have bought two new ones. Usually after a few days holed up in a motel, and with the new clutch or motor installed, we were ready to travel again. As many miles as we traveled though we were fortunate that vehicle breakdowns were all we had, along with only a couple minor fender benders.

Our emotional breakdowns were worse than our pickup breakdowns. At times we felt like we couldn't go on any longer and were tired of trying. Some days were so discouraging that we would question if it really was worth the effort. My medication helped me handle my husband's outbursts of rage even though it was hard at times. We had been told that trials were "hell" so we were absolutely sure that a trial with a bank was double hell. Then, after thinking about it for a while, we would decide it couldn't be any worse than what we had gone through that past year.

It was going to be a struggle, but we also had to think of our son and daughter, how hard they had worked supporting us. We had to look out for their future as well. We had to try and stay positive. We had to keep going—there was no alternative.

Look On the Bright Side

    This is the day we had been looking forward to. We sent the final check down to the attorney so he could start representing us, and this time we felt he was capable of the challenge. We certainly hoped so since he had required that much money up front. It was such a relief to finally have it done and have someone representing our side that we didn't quibble about his fee. All four of us celebrated that evening with pizza, chips and sodas—a real junk food celebration.
    What we didn't know at the time was that the bank's attorney had filed a request to the court for a summary judgment against us. Apparently they knew we had been without legal representation during that time, taking advantage of the situation while there was that window of opportunity. Luckily, as it turned out, we did have representation and just in time. What a relief to have somebody behind us, believing in us, listening to our side of the story and telling us not to worry. Even though it had been wearisome with lots of time and work involved, finally we felt relief. Every penny we could come up with went to this attorney, consequently other necessities had to be neglected. We still had no health insurance of any kind so feared getting sick or injured. Our trial wasn't scheduled until the next year so we had another full year to worry about it. We just added that to our list and lumped them all together. I guess we had hardened ourselves somewhat to the life of worry and risk. We didn't talk about the risk factor though since we pretty well had no choice—it was either continue on or give in. We had already paid the bank so much of our money when we paid off the loan, now all they could be

going after was our livestock, our champion cattle. They already had my home farm tied up and, of course, that old red pickup.

Our new attorney seemed confident that they had no right to any of our cattle since we had paid off our loan, so we continued to go out on the road selling to help with living expenses. Medication was helping my nerves, but by then I had developed such agoraphobia that I couldn't drive our car or leave home—only if someone took me. It was a terrible feeling of helplessness that didn't improve for two years. It was long after our trial was over before I could actually drive the car by myself.

Speak the Truth and Speak It Always, Cost You What It Will, for He Who Hides the Wrong He Does, Does the Wrong Thing Still

(Mom's favorite and most often used phrase)

    After three years of waiting, two years of preparation, and one year of nervous exhaustion, our day in court was getting close. Apparently that's when attorneys begin to work on their cases.

    Any prior discussion about the bank wanting to settle the case appeared to have been testing me, and was just a smoke screen to confuse the issue. Our attorney was pushing me more and more to accept the bank's offers of settlement. Since they had already sold my land, and we had paid off our operating loan, their offers didn't seem acceptable to me. To push me harder, our attorney was now telling us that it would be very difficult to recover anywhere close to the damages we were entitled to since it was a bank we were dealing with. He also reminded us that there was a good possibility we could lose if we took it on to trial. This was not what I wanted to hear from him, but it was starting to sound familiar. We reminded him that we couldn't be any more broke financially than we already were and that the hardest part for us had been coming up with his retainer he required to take our case. We had lost our health insurance and our life insurance, so we couldn't turn back. We had invested too much time and money.

In the meantime, I was persuaded to go over to the local mental health clinic to see about help for my nervous problems. I had never been to anyone like this before, but my counselor turned out to be great, easing my apprehension. She explained to me that until this mess with the bank was straightened out it would be hard for me to keep control over my emotions. I felt really foolish because I was certain there were many people with far worse problems, but she told me I could either come to visit with her, take medication, or go to the hospital. When she put it that way I was happy to visit with her each week. I tried taking some medication, but discontinued it when it caused reactions. On one visit my counselor told me I should speak to farm groups because I understood the farm situation so well. She thought I should share what I was going through with other farmers. It would have been a good thing for me to do, but I just didn't think I could handle the additional stress at that time.

"Maybe later," I told her. In fact, I was certain I couldn't handle it with everything else I had going on at the time. Had I done it, I'm afraid my comments regarding the farm manager from the land grant college would not have been very positive since he was heavily involved in forcing me to leave my home farm. He wasn't exactly my favorite person. I didn't see how he could work for the university, paid by the taxpayers, and then go out and give speeches to (widow farm owners) farm groups, then sign on to manage their farms for a fee. It always seemed like a two-sided sword to me, and I was on the wrong end of that sharp instrument. What the counselor had said to me did make me think though, so I started keeping a journal about what was taking place. Win or lose our case with the bank, it gave me more strength to get through those days getting ready and waiting for our day in court.

Time Waits for No Man

The trial was scheduled to begin at 9:30 a.m. the next day. It didn't take any alarm clocks to wake us up that morning—in fact, it didn't even take a call. Our family was up by at least 6:00 and the chores were done. After a small breakfast, even though it was hard to eat, we were all ready to go by 7:00. There wasn't even a lot of chit-chat, but more of an anxious anticipation of what was ahead for us.

We waited as long as we could, drove our old red pickup as slow as we could, parked two blocks away from the courthouse, slowly walked down the street, and still got there forty-five minutes early. It's hard to describe the feelings we felt during that time of waiting. Nervous, I'm sure, yet anxious to finally have the opportunity to tell our story. I was so excited I could have told everyone I met just what we were doing there that day.

As we sat and waited, the courtroom filled with prospective jurors. I was almost afraid to look behind me for fear one of them would be a familiar face. One little old lady came in and sat down by a fellow juror, saying, "Here we go again."

Her acquaintance replied, "I don't think this one will be like the others though." Hearing that, gave me a more secure feeling. It hit me with the reality that we were finally ready to begin. Our attorney soon came and told us to go over to the center area of the packed room and seat ourselves at the table. Normally during times like this my heart would be pounding through my chest, but for some reason it was not. I was extremely calm. My husband, on the other hand, was becoming more nervous. Three years of waiting, day after day of talking and thinking about the same thing, then with the time of decision getting closer his worries were starting to take over his thoughts. Times and dates were hard to remember anyway—it was like trying to cram for a semester test as a fifty year old. It really didn't matter if he got them confused as they were all written down on paper anyway, but he was starting to question our decision. Was our attorney right? I guess I had been practicing "calm" for days so it seemed to carry over for me that day.

The court bailiff called for everyone to rise as the judge for our case came from his chambers into the courtroom. I must say he was not what I expected. His hair was white, yet he didn't look old. He seemed to have a nervousness that was making me uncomfortable.

Across the large table where we were seated sat two opposing attorneys and a bank officer. All were spit and polished from the high gloss on their shoes to the gray pin-striped, three-piece suits they were wearing. They gave off a definite reminder that they in fact, were big city attorneys with more partners distributed in other parts of the room. In the front row of the audience sat two additional assistants. It could have been very intimidating, as I'm sure it was intended, but not that day. I knew we were in the right.

It seemed strange that the bank president was not there, but we didn't have time to find out why. It was time to take the jury poll and draw out the names. Dismissal excuses were heard—some potential jurors were excused. One lady brought her excuse to the courtroom with her: a two month old baby. She was the first to leave. After the twelve names were drawn, our attorney as well as the opposing attorney questioned each prospective juror. The final eight were selected, and we were ready to hear the opening statements from each side.

The judge made some request about us settling our dispute now and not taking the jurors' time, which we had been prepared to hear. His comments about the case and that there was question as to whether he would allow the jury to decide our case, however, we were not expecting to hear. I assume it was to put further pressure on us, which it did. We had waited three years for this day and he wanted us to dismiss it in thirty minutes. That was not an option as far as I was concerned.

Then he called all of the attorneys into his chambers to discuss the possibility of settling the claim. We were not invited. After their brief discussion, our attorney called us out to the hallway and told us that the judge was himself a rancher and that he would not allow any speculation testimony, that he understood the business and that he didn't think we had been damaged that much. The judge had agreed that the law was on our side in this case, but if it was allowed to continue the bank would suffer reputable damage. It seemed by his comments that we would no doubt win our case, but he did not want this to continue for the benefit of the bank's reputation. I was getting more upset as I listened to these pressure points since he didn't seem to care about *our* reputation—that we as the little guy had already been damaged a great deal. As a further hammer over us, he was putting a lid on any jury award. That was definitely last minute pressure. It seemed he was taking it completely out of the jury's hands, and I could not understand why, but I was fast losing my faith in our judicial system. Had the bank bought off the judge? I wouldn't think so, but it did cross my mind. The only question I could even think to ask our attorney in my state of shock was, "Will he be fair?" and I was told that he would be. I just responded, "That's all I ask. Let's go on."

The bank had made a token offer of settlement, and it was obvious that the judge had his mind made up that we should accept it even before he heard our case. This didn't impress me at all. I always thought our judicial system was a little more fair and understanding than this. So, we returned to the courtroom ready to begin, the jurors returned to their jury box when we were again called out to the hallway for a "final offer," which our attorney said we definitely should accept. It seemed that more of this trial was taking place in the hall than in the courtroom. The offers, much the same as before our trial even started, weren't anywhere close to covering the damages they had caused. Since I could see the stress on my husband from all of this, the offers were tempting.

I knew I had to be strong for everyone's sake, plus I was getting a little more disgusted with this entire process of last minute pressure so I told our attorney again that I was not going to accept it. The judge was getting angry with us, and the jury was waiting, but I didn't feel it was we who were holding up the trial. The attorneys were again called to the judge's chambers. It seemed like an eternity this time, but was probably more like twenty minutes. Our attorney appeared to also be getting disgusted because he came out of the chambers and said, "Let's go. We're gonna try this thing!" At last! Back we went to the courtroom, ready to go. The first witness was the bank official we had subpoenaed to testify. He was spotless. He looked like a little boy who had been dressed by his mother that day and sent off to Sunday school. His shoes were shiny, his hair was styled, his pants were creased, and his tie was so tight that his round cheeks puffed out on each side of his face.

Our attorney went to the front of the room and began to present opening comments to the jury. At that time, before he could even start his statements, the bank officers, bank attorneys, and the judge all ran back to the judge's chambers like it was a stampede. One bank officer scurried over to the phone. Then we were beginning to guess that the calls were being made to the bank president who had declined to attend. Once again we were called out to the hallway. This time we went into what they told us was a "continuance," and that it would be continued the next day in a different county.

Things weren't making much sense to us at that point, but we just hoped our attorney was being honest with us and looking out for our best interest. Our entire future was in his hands at that point. His last presentation to us was a ruling from the judge regarding a settlement. At the time we assumed this message had honestly been relayed to us through our attorney, but as time passed I wondered about that as well. There had been several times in the week prior to our trial that our attorney strongly encouraged me to include my farm in any settlement, but I refused because I didn't think it should be involved in our case regarding the livestock. I knew it would only complicate the matter since it was at that time tied up with my mother getting all of the income through life estate. In reality though, at some point in time at her death our attorney stood to make lots of money by including it.

The next day we did as requested and drove down to the newly appointed court. When our attorney arrived, I questioned him.

"What are we doing down here?" He only smiled and told me I had some papers to sign I guessed only that the three-year wait was about to come to an end—sort of an odd end. Why was there a change in counties? I didn't know, I didn't understand, and had no idea what all took place on that day. The bank had made an offer of settlement, with the exception that the judge had added to it. It had been such a long process. No amount of money could make up for all of the problems they had caused, but for the betterment of my family I agreed to the settlement. It was beginning to look like I had no choice.

Years later I learned a little more about the settlement and signing papers in a different county and why I was forced into the settlement as I was. This was another time and another struggle and many thousands of dollars in legal fees for me to pay, but when that time came I found out the entire truth. The attorney who was so diligently looking after our best interests was also looking after his own. Lessons can come at a high cost, but it was the best we could do.

Our family had gone through a tremendous struggle during those years. I'm sure everyone thought we would just give up the fight, and I'm sure many people would have. Tension was tight in our family at times as we seemed to start to go forward and then something else would happen to send it the other way again. We wondered how many negative things we could absorb and still keep our health. Frustration came out at the oddest times and places. I learned that I, too, had a breaking point even though I tried to remain calm. My counselor was right. After this was all over it seemed like a heavy weight had been lifted. I only saw her one time after that day in court.

I vividly recall the day I was finally able to drive by myself the twelve miles to our local town. I knew the exact halfway point, so once I passed that point it was either go forward or turn around and return home. I forced myself on this particular day to go forward. The last half of the trip was like a different planet to me. It was a blur of scenery—countryside that I had grown up seeing for fifty years, but it seemed as if I was seeing it then for the very first time. That day was a breakthrough for me. Gradually I increased my driving distance until I could drive twenty miles to the state capital. Once I was able to do that I could go ahead and look for work. Not completely sure of myself, I decided to go the shortest distance of about three miles and work in a nearby café. Never having done waitress work before, it was an entirely new learning experience. At times it was enjoyable, other times it was just a lot of low-pay hard work. Since my work hours were from five in the morning until lunchtime, I spent the afternoons making things to sell. Those were long days of work, so after a year I was definitely ready to try my luck driving further into the city.

At my age, work wasn't easy to find, especially with my outdated office skills. I had heard talk about computers—some good, some bad, but I realized that it was a necessity if I planned to get back into the work force. I enrolled in a computer college, taking the courses they offered. It was not easy to say the least. Every night I studied like I hadn't studied for years—probably never, but it was a great feeling of accomplishment when I completed it. I thought the schooling was the hard part, but I found that even with my new computer skills, good work at my age was difficult to find. I was determined though to find something other than waitress work again. When I did finally get hired to do secretarial work for an insurance company, I was so proud. A paycheck. I hadn't seen a real paycheck for years.

April Showers Bring May Flowers

The last visit:

"Well, Ms. Rae, how are you feeling today?" I hear as the door to my room opens. "I have your medicine ready now, but wouldn't you like to have a little snack brought in this afternoon? You know you haven't been eating like you should."

I am not hungry, she knows that. Besides, I'm going home today just as soon as I get dressed. I have two dresses hanging in my closet—I think I will wear the blue one. When the car gets here to pick me up I will have that sweet young couple get it out of the closet for me, then they can pack up my other belongings for the trip home.

It is going to be so grand to be back in my own home, sitting at the table with my family, discussing the farm work and the plans for the future. I'll just wait and have something to eat once I get there, so the nurse can just forget about me eating anything. I am not hungry.

Just as the nurse was leaving, I heard, "Hi, Mom" from somebody entering my doorway. A beautiful young lady, carrying a clear glass vase of purple violets, came into my room. Violets and roses have always been my favorite flowers. I know these are violets, but I'm not sure who is holding them. Is it somebody I should know and care for? My voice was just too weak to thank her as she sat the vase down on my bedside table. I hope she understands from my faint smile how much I love them.

"The spring flowers are blooming. Did you know that, Mom? It won't be long before the roses will be in bloom, too—your very favorite."

This vase of flowers makes me think about my son when he was just old enough to walk. He had picked me a beautiful bouquet of flowers, but he had picked them out of my flower garden, so I scolded him. How could I ever scold him for doing such a nice thing for me?

When my grandmother had a flower bed she raised bright orange poppies. They almost took over the farm much to the disgust of my granddad. Mom's flower garden was more traditional with red, pink and white peonies, purple phlox, purple and white lilacs, and white spirea. Out of necessity these were all easy to care for, not interfering with her busy work schedule.

In the back of our yard, a mass of multi-colored hollyhocks were in bloom all summer, then as winter approached they would drop their seeds to the ground for regeneration the next spring. I made dozens of hollyhock dolls during their peak blooming time, then I would line them up on the walkway as if they were little dancing dolls at the ball.

Mom also had a mock orange bush (one of the few things she purchased). This particular bush had the prettiest, sweet-smelling white flowers you could imagine. That bush stayed with the farm for as long as we lived there. When we moved away I took the bush with me to be replanted.

"Mom, would you like your bed moved so you can look out the window? The sun is shining today and the grass is getting green. It's starting to look like spring."

Oh, such a sweet young lady, and I know she is talking to me—I just don't understand what she is telling me. Should I know? Is she here to take me home now? Will she get my blue dress out of the closet for me to wear? Is she going to pack up all of my belongings? Did she bring the car? I think it may be too far to walk, but I'm not sure.

Then she and the nice young man pushed my bed over close to the window so I could again see outside of this lonely room, next to my window where once again I can see life. I can watch the children play and ride their bicycles. I can watch as they blow the white seed fluff from the dandelions or rub the yellow blooms on each other's noses after quizzing, "Do you like butter?"

I can watch them play in the mud puddles and make mud pies to cure in the warm sun, and I can see the tiny plants of corn starting to come up through the ground. Soon their appearance will create a solid green field that will remain all summer until once again the progression of nature turns it golden brown—ready for fall harvest.

That Old Time Religion

"We have to go back home now, Mom. Is there anything we can get you before we leave?"

As they walked out the door to the hall I knew it would be the last time I would see these caring young people who somehow, someway have been so very important to me in my life.

"We love you."

Then they slowly walked on out into the hall and out of sight as the door closed.

> *"Oh, how I miss the green grass scrunching under my feet*
> *And spring showers bringing in the fresh air so sweet.*
> *With the call of a robin as she builds her new home*
> *And the smell of new hay on the morning it's mown.*
> *I miss not knowing the past that I've had;*
> *The happiness I have shared—even the sad.*
> *God, if you're listening, please hear what I say*
> *I pray take me home to be with you this day."*

As my head dropped back down onto my pillow I could see only the wind churning the bare, dry soil into a screen of black. Like a dense fog, the darkening dust had completely covered my beautiful world outside my window. I can no longer see the grass meadow, only the fading red and purple of the sun as it disappears beyond the hills. The shadows of the tall pines slowly vanished until I could no longer see them in the distance. My cherished revelation of life had grown completely dark as I passed through my window.

PASSED THROUGH THE WINDOW ON MY WAY TO LIFE…

"It's me, oh Lord, I've passed through the window to life…"